Munira's
Bottle

Munira's Bottle

Yousef Al-Mohaimeed

Translated by
Anthony Calderbank

The American University in Cairo Press
Cairo New York

First published in 2010 by
The American University in Cairo Press
113 Sharia Kasr el Aini, Cairo, Egypt
420 Fifth Avenue, New York, NY 10018
www.aucpress.com

Dar el Kutub No. 13993/09
ISBN 978 977 416 346 3

Dar el Kutub Cataloging-in-Publication Data

Al-Mohaimeed, Yousef
        Munira's Bottle / Yousef Al-Mohaimeed; translated by Anthony
    Calderbank.—Cairo: The American University in Cairo Press, 2010
        p.   cm.
        ISBN 978 977 416 346 3
        1. Arabic fiction
        892.73

1 2 3 4 5 6   14 13 12 11 10

Designed by Adam El Sehemy
Printed in Egypt

Love, in its means, is war; in its foundation, it is the mortal hatred of the sexes.

—Friedrich Nietzsche

People, my ear is in love with a maiden in the hayy!
For sometimes the ear falls in love before the eye.

—Bashar bin Burd, blind Arab poet, 718–84

1

A cold morning in late February 1991. The sky is white and clear, undisturbed by the shriek of F16s. The city awakes, bleary-eyed. Pigeons leave their slimy droppings on the air raid sirens that perch atop government buildings. The bus engines on the town center route rumble into action along Olaya Avenue with thickly mustached Bedouin drivers, red headscarves thrown over their shoulders, grubby tagiyas cocked to one side. The Afghan bakeries slowly come to life with Pakistani and Indian workers who slip out of the narrow alleys and newly constructed side streets on bicycles decorated with plastic flowers. Indonesian and Filipina maids descend from their rooms on the roof to mop cold marble Rosa tiles and scrub stainless steel banisters. From downstairs rooms the voice of the Quran reciter, Abdul Baset Abdul Samad, floats from the radio sets of Najdi grandmothers as they intone, "Glory be to God" and wait for the smell of fresh coffee spiced with cardamom, which the Indian and Sri Lankan cooks prepare so well.

Alone in her room, Munira al-Sahi, unmarried, early thirties, lay in her large, comfortable bed. Her eyes were fixed on the ceiling, staring blankly like the eyes of the dead, as she went over the scandalous calamity of the previous night in her mind. "What was all that about?" she asked herself. Why all the deceit, the pretense that went on for all these months? How had he managed to work his way into her life with his false name and his made-up job, and the personality, family, and friends that were not his: a whole sinister world of deception?

1

She got slowly out of bed, leaning against the wall as she walked over to the pink curtains patterned with large white flowers. She drew them open and looked down at the street, the cars sleeping silently, before the rays of the sun strike the façades of the concrete buildings decorated with chiseled stone. The city yawned after a grueling sleep. The air raid sirens had fallen silent and the pandemonium of Soviet Scuds and American Patriots had ceased, but military vehicles and troop carriers still patrolled the streets at night. Munira's wonderful eyes were swollen from a night of weeping bitter tears. She and the city are very much alike: the city has a heart, and she has a heart too. The city has trees that look like a sad woman's hair. She has hair that resembles the trees in a desperate city. The city has eyes that watch everything, and she has eyes that contemplate. When she woke up, the guests had abandoned the party, leaving behind them silence and tables of leftover food and sarcasm and slanderous gossip. And so the city awoke; the American soldiers with their ammunition, light automatic rifles, and military uniforms had departed, leaving it to breathe freely and reflect.

The military left the city and he left the woman he loved. The foreign forces pulled out, leaving the city behind, and he lost her wide eyes with their provocative looks. He was a soldier with his weapon, and the remnants of many deceits lurked in his eyes. Munira al-Sahi had opened her heart as quickly as she now opened the curtains. A large spider with its pairs of spindly legs fell on the floor between her soft, bare feet. It was the latest spider to crawl across the plaster ceiling, one of the many that had flourished and thrived in her room over the last few months. Through the windowpane, whose edges had been taped up to stop gas seeping through in case chemical weapons were used, she looked at the Bengali cleaner in his yellow overalls as he swept up pieces of paper, empty drinks cans, and cigarette packets; stories and schemes and little conspiracies.

Her father's red GMC stood lazy and despondent under the huge sidr tree. The Bengali cleaner was sweeping up the leaves it had shed as it had wept through the night. The one who felt the defeat and the guilt and the failure most of all was her father. The instigator of the Mother of all Battles in Baghdad could hardly have felt more defeated or shamed as his armies withdrew from Kuwait than Hamad al-Sahi had felt the previous night when the treachery of his favorite daughter's fiancé was finally revealed. Because of her and her journalistic talent, he had lost his family and relatives, for he had resisted their demand that she omit the tribe's name from hers when it appeared in the newspaper. They had suggested she use a pseudonym but she had stubbornly refused, and her father had stood by her, delighted by her courage and resilience.

Through the shaded glass Munira noticed a pale and dismal moon fading in the sky above the city. In it she saw her shattered dreams buried alive together with her love, which had filled the streets, shops, restaurants, and cafés, from al-Takhassusi Avenue to Olaya Avenue, down Tahliya Street; from the Chinese restaurant to Maxime's Lebanese, as far as Café Roma and Patchi, the confectioner's. She would sit next to him in his car as they snuck around streets on high alert, waiting for the wail of the sirens, a stray Scud missile to scatter the darkness. His huge hand with its thick hair enveloped her small, soft hand with its pink painted fingernails and diamond eternity ring. She would slide her other hand across her lap and place it on top of his. Then her fingertips would work skillfully through the hairs on the back of his hand until he let out a deep moan, and moved his hand, with hers on top, to the gear stick of the white Jeep Cherokee.

On previous nights, when he had asked her to come out of the Young Women's Remand Center where she worked, she had been reluctant. She was supposed to stay with her colleagues on the night shift, looking after deviant young women who might come under attack from a stray missile. The curfew meant that the city was deserted at nights; nothing except army personnel carriers patrolling in threes, and jeeps driven by American soldiers, sometimes by female conscripts with their blond hair tied back like the tails of white horses.

"You know I have a permit to move freely at night."

He hoped he might persuade her to go for a quick drive so that he could steal a kiss from her tender lips and roam all over her body with his hands, as freely as he roamed from one end of the city to the other.

"I know. I have one too, but I can't."

Nevertheless they snatched some short times together, huddling like two bats in the family section at the Khuzama Center coffee shop, by the al-Nakheel restaurant on Olaya Avenue. He'd order her a cappuccino and hesitate over the menu every time but then always decide to have a Turkish coffee. He'd look into her bewitching eyes for minutes on end, take both her hands and lift them to his lips, one after the other, slowly, dreamily, while she basked in the attention, her head spinning. He tested her with a question about the difference between kissing the palm of the hand and kissing the back. She didn't know, so he explained:

"One of the classical texts says that kissing the back of the hand means I love you, whereas kissing the palm means I want you."

One evening he asked her: if he weren't a major and weren't single, but married with children and did some humble job, would she still love him, or associate with him?

"No!" she answered curtly, then shot back, "Why do you ask?"

"No particular reason. I just wanted to be sure you loved me."

They went into a long silence before his huge walkie-talkie crackled into life on the table. He picked it up, having heard the call on the F3 band, and informed the person on the other end that he was at work.

In her room Munira al-Sahi peeled the adhesive tape off the edges of the windows. She pulled hard at the glass and the aluminum frames rattled as clouds of dust flew up: "The war's over now," she sighed. It wasn't clear which war she meant. Desert Storm and its missiles, or the war for her heart and the storms it had endured, from her first infatuation with the lover to the bitter desolation she had reaped.

Munira had just finished reading the official verdict issued by the court, which had returned her social status to 'single,' as it had been prior to August 1990. It was as if no one had ever burst into her lonely heart. She thought for a moment how more had happened in those six months than in the previous thirty years of her life. She had won and lost a fleeting and tempestuous love. She had lost the opportunity to do her master's in social science after the university had revoked the contract of her supervisor. Dr. Yasser Shaheen, a Jordanian of Palestinian origin, had been sacked because of Jordan and Palestine's position on the invasion of Kuwait and their opposition to foreign troops coming into the region. She had lost her innocence and her ability to trust others, and her Siamese cat, Susu, now studied her actions and reactions in an effort to understand what had happened to her. She had even taken to observing the spiders that had been appearing on her ceiling since the 13th of last July, and the webs they wove to catch their weak and unsuspecting prey, which came buzzing along

5

with naive excitement until it fell into the trap and the spiders closed in: hapless victim cocooned in sticky threads.

Munira had given up her journalism as well, after her brother—who had come back from Afghanistan years before—raged at her, claiming that the scandal would never have happened had it not been for that column of hers, "Rose in a Vase," which appeared every Tuesday in the evening paper. And he blamed their father for not reigning her in and keeping her under tight control: "Women need a firm hand!" He said he would pulverize any seeds in her head that hadn't been crushed yet. He even confronted her father with the possibility that she might not be a virgin anymore, and if she were, then she should prove it and accept the first man to knock at the door.

She no longer left the house except to go to her work at the Young Women's Remand Center, and that she had had to fight for. Her brother Muhammad made it a condition that he would take her to work and bring her back home at lunchtime—and no evening shifts. So she would go into her room and close the door, draw the pink curtains with white flowers on them, and light a jasmine candle. From under her bed she would pull out some pieces of white paper with ornately patterned borders and write on them with a blue ballpoint pen. Then carefully folding up each piece of paper, like someone who had learned to roll their own cheap cigarettes, she would place them into an old bottle on which Indian designs were traced in silver, though they had mostly faded away with the touch of her hands over many years.

2

"If anyone tells a sad story I'll give her a present!" said Grandmother in her room on the ground floor. The window looked out onto the dead grass in the garden. Grandmother used to say that sad stories made the grass grow. She had decided that the eldest would begin, so my sister Nura thought a little then told the story of the horse possessed by a genie that had fallen in love with Ghazwa, the Bedouin girl. Every time it saw her it whinnied. All her brother Ghazi, the horse's owner, could do was to put her in a room over the horse's stable so it wouldn't see her and get excited. But the bewitched horse smelled her scent upstairs and began to bang the flimsy ceiling with its head until it had made a small opening and it could see the ravishingly beautiful Ghazwa. When this happened Ghazwa packed her belongings immediately and said farewell to her brother. Then, with her black slave girl by her side, the two of them ran away in fear. Every so often they turned to look back, and Mistress Ghazwa would ask her slave, "Can you see anyone behind us?" The slave peered into the shimmering desert with her keen eyes. "I see something, Mistress, the size of a pearl." They ran on for a while, then she asked her again and the slave answered, "I see something the size of a date." Mistress Ghazwa ran off again, dragging her exhausted slave behind her: "Can you see anyone behind us?" "I can see something the size of a rabbit." And then it was the size of a sheep. Mistress Ghazwa and her slave decided they should take refuge in a large acacia tree. Mistress climbed up first, taking her bundle of things, and then the slave joined her. It was only a matter of moments before the bewitched horse stood foaming beneath the tree, trying to get up. Then he started to dig beneath the tree so it would fall, until Ghazwa said to him, "My brother's horse, open your mouth and I will throw myself into it!" The horse opened its mouth and she threw down her abaya. The horse swallowed it but did not die. It began to kick the bottom of the tree again with its hooves. She repeated the command, "My brother's horse, open your mouth and I will throw myself into it!" The horse opened its mouth and she threw down a cooking pot. The horse devoured it and then raised its forelegs in order to climb the tree. Ghazwa took out her scissors and opened them as wide as they would go and tied the handles with a strip of cloth torn off the sleeve of her dress so they would stay open. Then she said for the third time, "My brother's horse, open your mouth and I will throw myself into it!" The horse opened its mouth and she threw down the scissors. They stuck in its throat even though it tried to swallow them like it had swallowed the other things, and it fell lifeless to the ground, after the scissors had torn its throat.

"Enough, please!" cried my grandmother and looked toward me indicating that it was my turn to tell a story. But my younger sister Mona interrupted, "Me, Grandmother! Let me tell a story." My grandmother smiled and nodded her head, indicating that we leave my story until last. Mona used her hands a lot while she told her story, especially when she was describing the girl who had fallen in love.

There was once a daughter of a tribal chieftain. Her name was Haya. She fell in love with a wandering poet whose name was Hassan. He loved her too and he described her beauty in all his poems. When his poems spread among the tribes, Haya's father decided to forbid her from leaving the house. Not just the house: he locked her in a room on the roof with just one window. The door was only opened to pass food in to her, and that was nothing but bread and butter. Hassan would stand beneath her window and recite his latest poems while she opened the shutters and looked down at him and together they would weep many tears. One day a conniving old woman, seeing Hassan weak and close to death, advised him to request his beloved to eat only half the butter and to rub the other half in her hair so that it would grow and grow, as she sang to it, "Grow longer my braids, grow longer." That way the lover would be able to climb up the braids to Haya's room. After some months Haya's hair had grown and she began to fold it by her side as if it were the body of a black man. Haya's mother noticed this and feared that there might be some trickery or betrayal afoot. She informed the father, who went to consult with the conniving old woman. The old woman suggested the solution. On the next pitch-black night when there was no moon, Hassan came to stand beneath the window of his beloved Haya. He threw a small stone and she opened the window, her hair at the ready. She had braided it into a strong, sturdy rope. As soon as she threw it down Hassan took hold of it, smelled it, and kissed it longingly. Then he grabbed on tight with his hands and began to climb with his feet set firmly against the wall. When he was almost at the window the conniving old woman appeared next to his beloved Haya, cackling loudly with her toothless mouth. She took out a huge pair of scissors and began to cut at the hair as Hassan called out for help and pleaded with her to stop. Haya wept and tried to free herself but someone was holding her tightly. Yes, it was her mother holding her. The conniving old woman snipped the last hair and Hassan fell to the ground and died before his beloved's eyes. Haya fell to the floor in a faint.

My grandmother smiled, revealing her gold tooth, and she nodded her head in appreciation of Mona's story. Then, silently, she turned to me and after a couple of seconds she said in a faint and melancholy voice, "Give us your story, ya Munira!"

3

There was once a woodcutter from Najd who had a wife he loved very dearly. She had borne him three daughters. When the youngest daughter was only three years old the mother died. The father was filled with grief. He avoided people and stopped working with his camel in order to dedicate himself to taking care of his daughters. But then people advised him to take another wife to look after his daughters, and to help him go back to his job as a woodcutter. So, after several months he married, for he had come to his wits' end and could not find a way of providing for his daughters. His new wife was extremely beautiful and he loved her dearly. But the stepmother, as in all the stories, was wicked and conniving. She was very jealous of the love the father felt for his three daughters, especially the little one, who shared their bed, and slept by her father's side, after he laid out his shmagh for her. She slept soundly when she could smell her father close to her. The stepmother started to become bored and annoyed with her husband and his daughters. Things came to a head and she gave him an ultimatum: either to divorce her or to abandon his daughters in the desert where someone else could find them and look after them. And because he loved her dearly and could not do without her, he agreed to do as she wished, on condition that he wait a whole year until his youngest grew old enough to go to sleep without him by her side. The stepmother agreed, but she could not take more than six months of it before she threatened him once again, her belly swollen with their first child. The woodcutter took his three daughters on his camel and set off into the desert. He had filled two pouches with food and drink. As the day's journey came to an end and darkness fell, the woodcutter halted his camel and took down his three daughters, who were delighted with the journey. He unloaded the food and drink and some woolen blankets and then falsely informed them that they would sleep there that night and in the morning they would all go back home. As usual the little one settled down on the woodcutter's shmagh, placed her tiny henna-painted hand on his chest, and fell fast asleep.

I noticed a tear slip from my grandmother's eye. She tried to hide it, while my two sisters could barely contain their grief at the tale. I continued.

After a third of the night had passed, the Najdi woodcutter had shed many tears as his chest rose and sank. He lifted the little girl's hand off his chest and stood up, wondering what to do about his head cloth, on the edge of which his favorite daughter was sleeping. In the end he took out the pair of scissors he'd brought along for this very purpose. He cut off the edge of the shmagh and took what remained. Then, wrapping it around his face against the desert cold, he incanted the name of God over his three daughters, covered them up, and left.

By this time the tears were not only flowing from my grandmother's eyes but my sisters Mona and Nura were crying as well. Mona was so moved that she hid her head between her knees and her little body trembled. Grandmother stood up and took a large bottle out of her cupboard. It had Indian designs on the sides and shining silver letters I couldn't understand. Inside were round colored sweets and as she gave it to me she said, "Keep this bottle. It might bring you some solace in your sadness."

After I'd shared the sweets with my sisters I kept the bottle and filled it with my secrets. It became my most trusted friend and never betrayed me. Everything that happened to me I wrote down and placed inside it. I told it all my troubles and problems but it never breathed a word to anyone, never complained about all the sadness and grief.

I remember when I was seven years old I caught a harmless black chafer. They look a bit like beetles but they eat grass. I was surprised they eat grass and I remembered what my grandmother used to say about how grass grows with sad stories. I told myself that the chafer's tummy must be full of grass and sad stories. Every time I put it in the palm of my hand its tiny legs would all walk and tickle me, and because I laughed so much it fell off the edge of my hand onto the sand. I kept it, though, and shoved it into the bottle so it would fill up with stories. But then it died. I turned the bottle upside down so the chafer would fall out, but it was no use. I cried a lot until my mother suggested breaking the bottle and I jumped up in horror and refused.

My grandmother took the bottle, having convinced me that she would tell the chafer some cheerful stories so its legs would move and it would come out. Next morning Grandmother gave me the bottle back and the harmless black chafer was nowhere to be seen. I didn't know whether she'd told it a happy story or a sad one and it had moved, or if she'd crushed it up with a knitting needle and thrown the powdered remains of its little body into the garden with the dead grass.

"Don't put live things in here to die," said Grandmother as she handed me back the bottle, wagging her finger in my face. "Put in dead stories so they can come alive."

4

I wish I hadn't been alone at home the night of 13 July 1990. If someone else had been there, none of this would have happened. If only I hadn't been so concerned about my research that I'd stayed in. If only I'd given myself the chance to go out for a while with the family and taken a drive in the car and we'd all gone to Hardee's. I'd have ordered one of those hot apple pies I liked and sat with my sister Mona at the table that looks out onto the car park and we'd have made our usual sarcastic comments about the boys showing off while we watched them from behind the darkened glass. How I wish Mona had stayed at home with me. She'd have seen to the pestering phone as she usually did and I wouldn't have had to answer. But it wouldn't stop ringing and the ringing became a long rope that slowly tightened around my neck over the following months until it strangled me.

I wish the phone hadn't rung that night, or that the volume switch had been on low and I hadn't heard it. I wish I hadn't interrupted the sentence I was writing: ". . . and from the perspective of social behavior it is clear that the suppression of delinquent young women's impulses . . . ." If only I hadn't stopped and put the pen to one side to answer the phone as it neighed. For it really was a neigh, announcing the arrival of a knight in shining armor, horse rearing up on hindlegs:

"Good evening."

"Hello."

"Oh. It seems I have the wrong number."

I put down the receiver gently. It was covered in soft material the shape of a bear's paw. I returned to my thoughts, intending to finish off the truncated sentence but I couldn't find my pen. It had white thread wrapped around it and three cheap beads at the end. It was a present from my friend Nabeela and I was really fond of it. I looked through my papers, on the bed, behind the bedside cabinet where the phone was. That's when it rang again. The galloping white stallion had returned.

"Excuse me."

"Yes!" I said brusquely.

"Am I taking up your time? Have I scattered your thoughts?"

"Excuse me? What do you think you're playing at?"

"I want you!"

"Who are you? Do you know me?"

"Of course I do."

And that's how he trotted in on his white charger, moving on without further ado into the subject of writing, and the textures I wove with my words in my column, "Rose in a Vase," every Tuesday in the evening paper. He turned out to be an avid reader, intelligent, perceptive, with an ability to predict the future. He was a good talker and his voice made the bear's-paw handset heat up in my hand. I felt the bear itself with his brown fur stretched out on my bed, embracing me in the softness of his thick coat, and I turned into a child in his arms, desperate for a warm embrace.

He said many kind things. He offered his opinions of writers and journalists and recited romantic poetry by Nizar Qabbani. He took me by the hand like a blind girl and led me through the constellations and galaxies of another universe. He wouldn't hang up and we chatted and whispered for more than an hour, before he promised he would call at the same time the following evening. Mother came back from her outing in a real state. They had tried to call me a dozen times to see what I wanted to eat but the line was constantly engaged and they were worried. I don't think I appeared too anxious but my eyes darted about a bit when I told her, "Susu must have knocked the phone off the hook and I didn't notice." Poor cat! There's no one but you to blame for my misdeeds. No one's picking on you, darling. I don't mind if you knock the phone off the hook, knock a glass off the table, or scratch a smart American sofa. I wouldn't even mind if you jumped over the wall and met a street cat and he took you for a walk outside the quarter and made love to you in a garden or a rubbish cart. I don't envy you, Susu dear. I'm just thinking about your freedom to enjoy your rights in full.

On the night of 13 July 1990 I was wearing a silk nightdress, pale green, with two fine straps of pure silk over the shoulders. Even so, I still had the air-conditioning turned up full. The heat was unbearable, and for the first time in years Susu didn't sleep with me. I didn't shoo her away or call her over, but she curled up in the far corner of the room and peered at me dejectedly through half-closed eyes. Did she know I'd blamed her for my misbehavior and accused her of being careless and clumsy? Or did she feel that my bosom didn't belong to her any more, and was no longer a warm, safe place for her to rest?

On subsequent nights he told me that of all the writers whose words adorned the pages of the evening newspaper, I was the most beautiful. He said my words were like small moons. He said I could see the good things in the harshest of situations. "You are no normal woman," he whispered. "You are a wonder. You are depths unfathomed, a deed unexpected, a moment of blinding revelation, and with a flutter of your eyelash you shatter the moon into a million moons." He loved Nizar's poetry. He had it committed to memory, and when he recited it my body tingled and I was like a child who just happened to be in her early thirties.

I put down the bear's-paw receiver and floated around the room like a princess in her private wing: pastel-colored walls and a white bed with a white rose-patterned bedspread; above it a canopy of the same material, and to either side an oriental painting—one of men and women holding drums and a woman dancing in front of them, the other of the white flash on the head of a jet black mare.

The only slightly disconcerting thing on that night I first heard his sweet voice was that when I lifted up the pillow to tidy the bed, I found a small insect. I looked closer and saw it was a spider that was calmly and confidently working its way under the edge of the pillow. I wondered at the time what it was doing there in my room. I blew at it, then made a cone out of one of the pages of my research, intending to catch the spider inside and toss it out of the window. But every time I tried, it managed to slip out again and crawl down the outside of the cone onto my hand. That made me jump and drop the cone. I thought of calling in the Filipina maid, Lillian, to help me get rid of it, but the little spider crawled slowly and deliberately up the wall toward the false plaster ceiling and disappeared. Over the following nights it would issue forth like a religious policeman, examining its soft silky threads, looking for any prey that might have become entangled in its trap. This clever strategy impressed me, although it went a long time without catching a fly or insect. Eventually I stopped watching it.

When I climbed into bed on the night of 13 July, it was just after midnight. I was treading that fine line between sleep and wakefulness, my eyes more or less closed but my mind still alert. I saw him—Ali, he had told me what his name was—standing in the doorway. The upper part of his body was normal but the lower part was shimmering and misty, fading gradually to nothing, as though he were the genie of the magic lantern. He was standing exactly where he would really stand a few months later, after managing to sneak into the house late one night and come up the stairs as if he knew just where my room was. He closed the door behind him quietly and embraced me. I felt as if I would dissolve like hot air between his strong arms. He covered my mouth with passionate kisses and led me with studied and practiced steps toward the bed. He was bold and impetuous. I was a ripe fig—as he described me later—ready to burst open, waiting for a trained fruit-picker. His experienced hand explored my breasts under the soft silk nightdress. Everything inside me awoke. I was in a state of total readiness. So was he. His thing was long and full and I felt its hardness as he threw me violently onto the bed. Suddenly, as I lay there on top of the bedspread, a distant childhood memory flashed into my mind, and I pushed him away. I stood up gasping for breath. The image of my friend Salma on their farm at al-Kharj as she tried to extricate herself from the grip of their strong young neighbor would not leave my mind. He had thrown her into a patch of flowering clover and all I could do, at fourteen years of age, was to shout and throw stones at him. Then I ran away for fear that he would catch me and do the same to me. Nevertheless, even now I don't know if she really was trying to get away from him or whether she was just pretending, to make him more forceful and violent. When I saw her a few days later her cheeks were rosy and she seemed refreshed and invigorated. At that point I felt she had known him before. But I was still overcome with a feeling of horror and it surrounded me like a wall whenever anyone tried to kiss me or get physical.

5

When it came to love and kisses, I was an apprehensive and reluctant novice. My workmate Nabeela was always flirting with me and never missed a chance to touch me. She'd come up and pour out all the problems she was having with her mother and her stepfather, and she would cry whenever she mentioned her real father, who'd died before she was six. I would hold her in my arms and comfort her as the weeping reached a crescendo and she would squeeze me as if she didn't want to let go. I put it down to the intensity of the moment but then she began to take things a bit too far.

Whenever I entered my office, I'd discover that she'd already been in and put some jasmine, whose fragrant scent I loved, on my desk. "Don't you think you're overdoing it a bit?" I'd say coyly, and she'd answer with a sigh, "But my day doesn't begin until I see you." I considered it a pleasant compliment from a colleague and nothing more, until she made a move that morning long ago.

We had just come back to work from the holidays but she wasn't there to shake my hand and wish me a happy Eid with the other girls. She'd arranged it so she could corner me when we were alone in my office. She hugged me tightly and kissed me on both cheeks. Her breath was so hot that it gushed into my pores and almost burnt my face. Even so I refused to get drawn into her sensitive domestic issues, preferring to maintain a certain distance.

She had told me once that she was fifteen and a bit when her mother and three sisters by her real father went out shopping for some clothes and perfume with the driver. They left Nabeela at home to study for her geography exam the following day. She was lying on her stomach on the bed, swinging her bare legs in the air, her attention alternating between the map of Egypt and its borders in the textbook and the fourteen-inch TV set as it broadcast the adventures of Nazik al-Silahdar in the soap opera *al-Hilmiya Nights*.

"During a particularly intimate moment between Safiyya al-Emari and Yahya al-Fakharani," she related, "my stepfather, who I'd learned to call 'father,' as my three sisters did, came into the bedroom. His face was swarthy and still bore the marks of some old pox, and he had a light beard. He didn't give me the chance to get up or greet him. He just jumped on top of me, horny and incoherent, snorting like a bull. He lifted up my green housedress, which had branches and two birds embroidered on the front and started to do me from the back. I passed out. I came round to feel something hot splashing on my back and saw him slinking away like a thief. That was the first time. There were lots of others. He would stay home, making excuses about needing to finish off the papers and reports he brought home from the ministry. My mother and sisters would go out shopping with the driver and I'd be in the house alone with him—his property that didn't talk back.

"Every time I look at the green dress, even after all these years, it amazes me how the two birds are looking in opposite directions whereas before they stood facing one another on two branches. I used to wonder who had undone the original gold embroidery and stitched it again so that each singing bird was averting its eyes from the other. If you don't believe me, darling, I'll bring it in tomorrow, here to the office, my green dress, and you can judge the position of the two birds for yourself. I swear they've moved from where they were before. That day time stood still as Safiyya and Yahya whispered to one another on *al-Hilmiya Nights*."

Nabeela spoke to me at length about her naive mother, and how she had helped her stepfather look at her body when they traveled to the Eastern Province and stayed in a rented chalet. She let the girls, including Nabeela, wear bathing suits and go in the swimming pool. They swam about like well-trained dolphins, supple-bodied, while the stepfather sat next to their mother smoking his sheesha, sucking the smoke through the mouthpiece and blowing it into the air as he watched the innocent adolescent girls. The mother pointed at Nabeela. "Look at Nabeela," she said innocuously to him. "She's grown up, her body's filled out." Stepfather puffed the apple-flavored smoke and ogled the apples of Nabeela's chest.

The first time Nabeela spoke to me about the situation, she broke down in my office. I stood up and closed the door so that the other women—the social workers, psychologists, and inmates—wouldn't notice. As I went back to her, she got up off the chair as if she were about to leave. She was sobbing and I had to ask her to stay with me in the office until she felt better. She took the opportunity to throw her body against mine and she hugged me tightly as she wept. I stroked her hair tenderly and felt her hot, panting breath on my neck.

One time I learned that Nabeela had refused a trip to Amman to take part in a seminar about how to encourage families to adopt foundlings and homeless children, although the subject interested her immensely. I asked her about it, as I thought it would have been a professional opportunity for her. She told me that her stepfather would be traveling with her as mahram. He had done the same thing two years before when she had gone to Abu Dhabi. He had stayed in the same hotel, in a separate but adjoining room. He kept knocking on her door at night like a passing traveler who comes in looking for sustenance and warmth, then departs satiated—victorious and guilt-ridden at one and the same time. He never looked directly into her eyes and ran away in the mornings, leaving her to attend the seminar.

The following year, when another opportunity came for her to attend a festival in Manama, Nabeela approached her brother Ahmed. His mustache was just sprouting and light hairs were appearing on his cheeks. She convinced him to go with her and he convinced the mother. It was a huge shock to the stepfather, who had dreamed of being alone with her, far away from unexpected interruptions.

Some months later the stepfather, as a result of his many connections in the city, managed to arrange for Ahmed to go and study in America. After Ahmed's departure the stepfather became the only mahram authorized by the mother to travel with Nabeela and look after her, and make sure she was okay when sleeping in five-star hotel rooms and not being subjected to the unwanted attentions of strange men.

Nabeela's eyes were like candles when she told her story, their light flickering every time she mentioned a trauma in her life, the tears sliding slowly down her cheeks like drops of melted wax. Despite all this she enjoyed moments of great joy and delight. She'd come to work in the morning dressed in gorgeous clothes, with three fresh jasmine flowers in her small handbag. She'd remove the day-old flowers before they were fully wilted and replace them with the new ones. Then she'd look at me, wink provocatively, plant a kiss on the palm of her hand, and blow it toward me, whispering, "May your morning be jasmine, most beautiful rose in the world." And I'd smile politely and give her a lukewarm reply.

One morning, as she placed the jasmine in the blue vase, she looked at me amorously, and her eyes seemed to linger on my necklace. It was made of white gold and on it hung a shining green emerald. It was a very attractive and alluring stone. My father had given it to me for my thirtieth birthday. Nabeela walked around the back of my desk, overwhelmed by the jewel. "Allaaaaah!" she gasped, her mouth agape in awe. Then she turned my swivel chair around so that I was facing her and brought her face close to mine, as if she were inspecting the emerald. Suddenly she took my heavenly face—which she called 'full moon rising'—firmly between her dark hands and pressed her mouth with its two protruding front teeth against my delicate lips. I slapped her without thinking and she rushed out of the room, sobbing silently.

The sharpness of those two teeth, which stuck out so noticeably, stayed on my lips for days. Apparently she had not broken the habit of sucking her thumb until she was twenty. She confided in me once that she was unable to get to sleep unless she had put her thumb in her mouth and sucked it silently until she dozed off. Nabeela had experienced great anxiety and instability in her life. She lacked the affection of her mother and her real father and her thumb provided her with peace and security when she slept.

After the slap Nabeela no longer held my fingers when she passed me a pen or some perfume. She no longer came into my office unless work demanded it, and when she did she entered broken and defeated. In the end I felt desperately sorry for her. Every day my conscience leaped up on my desk like a genie sitting in judgment. In the end I made it up to her with a bottle of the new fragrance from Oriental Woman.

6

Whenever Nabeela ranted and complained about her mother's husband, I would ask her why she didn't threaten to tell her mother about his secret habits. That way he might stop abusing her. But Nabeela was sacrificing herself for the sake of a perfect home and a stable family. The mere insinuation that there was anything going on would bring the house crashing down and shatter its tranquillity.

How many women live such silence, I wondered; and was Ali al-Dahhal—that was his full name—who had, on the evening of 13 July, smothered me with loving words, poems, and passion, just like all those other men? Was he secretly laying a trap for me?

Why is my father so understanding, thoughtful, and kind? Is there no one else like him in the world? True, he's simple and doesn't think much. In fact he doesn't like to think too much so he won't open himself up to situations he can't control. I remember, on 17 January, running down the marble stairs to my father and standing there out of breath:

"The war's started."

He looked up quietly from the daily accounts book of the perfume and incense shop he owned in al-Deira, then turned his eyes back to his papers.

"The first air raids have taken off from Dhahran," I added.

He crossed out a line and wrote a comment in the margin in his shaky, illegible handwriting, then turned the page. "The sheikhs know best," he said without looking up.

I went back up to my room, climbing the stairs silently as I thought about my father's ability to control his emotions, and his coldness, which clothed the walls of the house in an insipid yellow.

My father didn't seem to care about a thing. He didn't doubt people's intentions or behavior. He never took a position on anything. He loved everybody, saw no faults in anyone. I could never work out if he ignored other people's faults or if he just didn't see them.

When Ali made an appointment to see my father to discuss the engagement, he was almost an hour late when he finally knocked on the men's door. While my father did not mind his coming late, I was furious. I told him off over the internal telephone. He apologized with sweet, romantic words that sent the angels in my head reeling, and my anger disappeared. Ali took his place at the head of the men's majlis and enchanted my father with his conversation, his ideas, and his common sense. His fingers played with a string of pearl prayer beads. He appeared to know everything, to plan for all eventualities, and to read the mind of the person he was talking to. He spoke about politics and economics and society and religion and philosophy. But in everything he talked about, he knew only the subject headings. From everything he read he took only the surface without appreciating the thing in depth. Whenever he encountered someone who was well-versed in a subject and who tried to draw him in and pin him down, he'd wriggle out of it. He was gifted with an extraordinary canniness.

When he took me by the hand on the evening of 13 July, he chose to talk to me about the subjects of my column, "Rose in a Vase." I found myself spellbound, being led along, submissive and compliant. There is no easier way to lead someone into a trap than to wax lyrical about that person's successes, to drown them in a lake of their own narcissism. Was I vain and naive? Do I only love myself? My sister Mona said I did. I'd put up some pictures of myself in my room. I had them done at the al-Atheer Women's Studio. The Filipina photographer had taken more than forty-six color photos of me and sent the negatives to be developed in America. It had cost more than five thousand riyals. These are my pictures, in quality silver frames all over the walls: in this one I'm standing next to a large urn, and there reclining on a couch with colorful Bedouin textiles in the background. In another I have the end of a pen resting at the corner of my lips. I look embarrassed by the flash.

I even have my picture engraved on the tiles in my bathroom. A Filipina woman who works at the Young Women's Remand Center told me about her friend who worked with ceramics and could draw on tiles. I asked her to get him to make me four twenty-square-centimeter tiles, which I had left over from when the walls were tiled. They were a lemon color and he painted my picture on them in burnt umber. I would place some scented candles around the edge of the jacuzzi, relax in the tub brimming with water and foam, and look at my precisely executed picture on the tiled wall.

Ali's words had amazed me and tempted me to continue the conversation, just as he had amazed my father with his knowledge of all subjects on his first visit. He had even spoken with my father about the different kinds of coffee and which was the best, and they had discussed the merits of American and Pakistani cardamom. In fact, they had even talked about scented woods and oriental incense and perfumes, after Ali had placed the incense burner between the hanging edges of his shmagh and enthusiastically inhaled the Cambodian incense. "Your incense smells wonderful, Uncle."

My father was delighted with Ali and he gave his consent in principle, on condition that he would inquire into his background. But my father did not inquire too thoroughly. The name of Ali al-Dahhal and his rank of major were well known to many.

One day, Father decided to visit him in his office at the ministry. When he stood in front of the office manager asking to meet Major al-Dahhal, he announced his name as if he knew him well:

"Tell him it's Hamad al-Sahi."

The manager mentioned Father's name over the telephone, and the Major asked him to wait until he finished the meeting he was chairing. Father sat down on a black leather sofa and looked for a moment at the photographs on the wall before shifting his glance to the wonderful pattern on a small Iranian rug. Suddenly he remembered he had an appointment with the traveling carpet merchant at the souk in al-Deira, who sold his rugs and carpets to eminent persons for many times their value, and who was going to introduce my father to his clients so he could offer them the scented Cambodian woods for fabulous prices. He got to his feet and left, with the intention of visiting my fiancé another time. Good Lord! How could Father walk out when he was only a stone's throw from the scandal? If you'd only stayed a few more minutes you'd have gone in to meet him, and we'd have resolved the issue early, before that disastrous evening ever happened—wouldn't we, Father?

It occurred to me, as I recalled a host of different situations, that fate is heavy and resounding. No one can avert it. Fate is like a parachutist who jumps out of an airplane at twenty thousand feet and when he tries to open the parachute it malfunctions. He keeps trying but the damn thing won't open and he hurtles toward the earth, heavy, unswerving as a stone, to crash inexorably into a very small patch of ground, no larger than one square meter. I was that square meter, and the parachutist falling like a stone was fate. Was there not, at the decisive moment, a hand to intervene, to untangle the rope so that fate and the parachute floated slowly to the ground and I could jump out of the way? I began to include in my prayers the request, "O Lord, I do not ask you to deflect destiny from me, but to be easy with it."

Father's philosophy on life was "God wishes us well." He would utter these words to resolve an issue, to end a gathering, or even if he were alone thinking to himself. But if he sensed some evil about him, or if he happened to get involved with evil people who got him into trouble, and he realized it was they who had done it, he would let out a deep, slow sigh and say, "God preserve us from the evil of those who have evil in them."

Father didn't like to get involved in matters that didn't concern him, or so he claimed. He didn't follow politics and he wasn't concerned with what was going on in the country. He wasn't even bothered about the latest developments in the oriental perfume and incense business. He stuck to his own blends and didn't mix with the other merchants. His small shop in al-Deira, next to the clock tower, hadn't changed in thirty years. He hadn't even replaced the black sign over the entrance that read "Hamad al-Sahi for Scented Woods." When he wanted to involve my brothers in his business he hired an Egyptian laborer to go up a stepladder, white paint dripping from the brush in his hand, and write under his name "and Sons."

Father never disagreed with anything, and never argued about anything. When the local council issued an order to demolish the perfume and carpet shops in the old area to make way for a new shopping mall, lots of the old merchants rejected the proposal and wrote a petition, but my father just repeated his famous line: "The sheikhs know best."

Father was Grandmother's only son. He had stayed at home by her side all the years of his childhood. She protected him from people and from the evil eye, even from the wind. She said that if the wind got inside one's head, one would never be the same again. Once, when they were younger, some of his friends persuaded him to go with them on one of the trading caravans destined for Palestine and Syria. He sneaked out of the house before dawn. When Grandmother found out, she lost control and ran after him and the camel caravan. She implored them to give her her son back. She didn't want him traveling. When she got no response, neither from them nor from him, she stood by the edge of the old Saheem well and threatened to throw herself in. "All I have in the world is my baby Hamad," she screamed. Then Father turned around and rode back, convinced in the end that it was for the best.

7

Grandmother, whose little face was scarred from smallpox, had been bedridden for years. She only ever left her room carried on a stretcher of sturdy canvas with two wooden handles. Her mind was crammed with stories, proverbs, and anecdotes. Her narrow eyes sparkled with joy whenever she found her son Hamad al-Sahi joining her for coffee at sunset, or in the morning immediately after the dawn prayer.

One evening toward the end of January, after the war had broken out and the weather was cold and gray, Hamad went into her room and found her trying to shoo something unseen from above her. At first he thought there was a fly buzzing around her head, or a mosquito that wouldn't leave her alone, but he couldn't see anything. Meanwhile she kept on waving her hands and muttering.

"What are you doing, Mother?" asked Hamad.

"I'm shooing away the angel, darling," she replied, still moving her arms.

Days later, as overwhelming sadness weighed down on Hamad al-Sahi's brow, he found his aged mother had placed one of her many pillows against the wall next to her.

"Who moved that from under your head?" he asked in astonishment.

"Where?" she replied, without looking into his eyes.

"There," he said, as he pointed toward the pillow. Grandmother looked at the pillow resting up against the wall, and asked it with a laugh: "What's the matter, Abu Hamad?" The pillow did not reply, though the eyes of Hamad al-Sahi did as their lids quietly and painfully closed. He mopped the tears with the edge of his shmagh as he left the room.

Munira was unable to stem the flow of tears from her wide eyes or to still her grieving heart as it thrashed about like a bird frantically flapping its wings. Grandmother didn't understand what Munira was doing when she tried to clean the old woman up. She had urinated and soiled the cotton bedspread that covered the plastic sheet they had placed underneath her. Grandmother looked at her out of one eye, having lost the vision of the other to a cataract.

"Where's Abu Hamad?" she asked, laughing heartily as she turned her face toward the window and sang in a soft mellow voice:

I laugh with those who laughed before me,
Though troubles they abound,
Now I'm wrung dry like a Bedouin's water skin,
I don't think I'll stick around.

On the last day Grandmother let out a great sigh. Her son Hamad found her standing with great difficulty, looking out the window into the yard. She was watching the drops of rain as they fell gently onto the roof of the GMC and splashed the leaves of the bougainvillea, whose fiery flowers with their triple petals climbed up the wall and poured over into the street. Her son Hamad was amazed and asked who had stood her there and how, after years of paralysis and confinement to her bed, she had managed to walked over to the window. He rushed toward her and grabbed her trembling hand, intending to take her safely back to her bed.

"Patience, my child," she said with a tear in her eye. "Let the rainfall be the last thing to delight my eyes. The grass in the garden is already dead, see. The rain won't make any difference."

Hamad shuddered as he stood next to her tiny crooked frame, and straightened her black shawl that hung down to her knees. He watched her follow the raindrops as they began to fall more heavily and lash the tiles in the yard. Her eye, covered with a light film of white, blinked in time with the demented drops as they hurtled to the ground. Then calmly, quietly, she closed her eyes and passed into a deep sleep, her head falling limply across her chest. She was like a basket of straw when Hamad lifted her in his arms and declared, "We belong to God and unto Him we return."

Munira and her mother stayed by the body while Hamad al-Sahi went out in his GMC to look for a corpse washer. He steered his car with some difficulty through the narrow alleyways in the old quarter of al-Atayef before pulling up by a green iron gate, its paint peeling off. He tapped on the gate three times with his key. Eventually he heard the voice of an old woman croaking intermittently in the distance, as if it came from the depths of a long-abandoned tomb.

"We have a funeral, old woman."

"Where?" asked the voice behind the door.

"In our house."

The old woman apologized, telling him to take the body to a mortuary at any mosque and she would join him there, undertake the task for the sake of God, and not require any payment. As for the houses of people she did not know, she would not enter them.

One of the hardest things for a person to do is to renege on a promise. How much more so if the promise has been made to a dying person, and not just to any dying person, but to the light of one's eye and the closest to one's heart. I want to be washed at home, prayed over in the Imam Mosque in al-Deira, and buried in the cemetery at al-Oud. These were her three conditions, and she always followed them with a request that was not as binding:

"Perhaps you'll be the one who lays me in my grave."

This last sentence, more akin to a prayer, was her fourth instruction.

Father came back in a state of consternation. What was he supposed to do with his mother's corpse, for he was adamant it would not be leaving the house until it had been washed and dressed in its shroud. He would have to take his wife with him to the old woman, the washer of corpses, so she could persuade her to come with them to their house. The wife suggested that he take his mother's corpse to the mosque to be washed quickly before the afternoon prayer, but Munira had seen how her grandmother had yielded to death. Her face had remained as it always was and hadn't become distorted or taken on a look of fear. Munira felt that this look of composure had only come about because she'd died at home. The corpse washer would have to come to the house. "She won't leave until she's been washed, anointed with perfumed oil, and put in her shroud," she insisted. So Munira's father and mother hurried off together. The streets were almost deserted, for minutes earlier air raid siren had gone off. They noticed a pale light to the south of the city and the sound of a distant explosion.

Mona kept out of sight in a room upstairs, sobbing uncontrollably, while Munira stayed by the door of her grandmother's room. She couldn't take her eyes off the body, laid out on the bed under a brown woolen blanket. She stared at the hand sticking out from under the blanket. Her heart thumped, and her wide eyes fluttered with fear. All of a sudden the phone rang. She screamed, then heard the voice of her beloved Ali al-Dahhal on the other end of the line. She burst into tears as she frantically told him the details of her grandmother's death.

As soon as Munira spoke his name, her grandmother's index finger began to twitch in a gesture of disapproval and irritation, but it was unable to conspire with Grandmother's cold palm and reach out to snatch the receiver from Munira's hand.

His voice comforted her, and his tender, understanding words soothed her troubled mind.

As Munira spoke, her eyes remained fixed on Grandmother's face, and she felt sure it was losing its serenity and had begun to scowl. She suspected this was because she was neglecting her grandmother and thinking more about her lover at such a sensitive moment.

A large number of men came into the yard through the main gate, led by Uncle Ibraheem. The scent of incense preceded them and butterflies of sadness fluttered above them, alighting upon their heads for a moment then dancing with astonishing agility across a small puddle of rain that had accumulated where the flagstones sunk into the ground. No one knew if they were sad for an old grandmother who had gone to her eternal rest, having soothed her exhausted eyes with the splash of the rain, or if their sadness and despondency were due to the Angel of Death, who had not yet gathered his wings from Grandmother's dress and was looking among the mourners for another face whose nostrils he could plug, snuffing out the flame of life.

An old woman came in wearing a long green dress with orange embroidery at the neck and cuffs. She took Grandmother's body in her henna-painted hands and set earnestly about her business as a washer of corpses. She placed the cold body on a low aluminum table that stood just a few centimeters above the kitchen floor, and doused it thoroughly with water from the hose pipe. Then she took out some small bottles filled with oils of musk, mustard, and camphor and began to anoint the body and pray. The sound of the prayer and the scent of the oils filled the kitchen and drifted out through the window to float into the sky and mix with the smell of gunpowder and shells.

The corpse washer hadn't gotten in the GMC with Father, even though his wife was with him. She followed them in another car with the son of her deceased sister. She sat in the back seat, while the eyes of the sister's son followed Father's license plate through the deserted streets, as the city waited for another Scud to screech across the distance from the northern border.

8

Father, Uncle, and the rest of the men carried off Grandmother's coffin. The corpse washer stayed with us in the house to offer her condolences. Meanwhile her sister's son, who, according to my brother had a long scar on his left cheek, went with the men to pray over Grandmother and bury her in the al-Oud Cemetery, as she had enjoined my father so many times.

As I brought in pressed dates and Arab coffee, I couldn't help sensing the triviality of modern life, now that my grandmother was gone. She'd argued with me right up to the end. She accused the girls of my generation of being naive and superficial, incapable of handling responsibility. She used to say that as soon as we felt any movement in our wombs we'd run in panic to a doctor's surgery or the hospital. She on the other hand had given birth ten times, and only four babies had survived, two boys and two girls, and she'd never been to a doctor, male or female, in her life. She said that she once felt the contractions coming on while she was working in a patch of clover, cutting the flowering heads with her sickle. She put down the sickle, concealed herself between the shoots of clover, gave birth, and cut the umbilical cord with the blunt edge of the sickle.

As I served the coffee I couldn't help feeling a twinge of resentment toward this woman who had delayed Grandmother's funeral because she refused to get into father's car even though my mother was with them. But before she had drunk her first cup, she turned to my mother and apologized for her lack of cooperation. My mother was very polite, though she also pointed out, "But my presence as a woman with my husband is enough." The corpse washer let out a sigh that caused the blades on the ornately carved wooden ceiling fan to shudder slightly.

"You don't know," she said, and her stern face looked all around the sitting room as she repeated, "You don't know what can happen.

"I live in a small single-story house in al-Atayef Quarter," she related. "Abu Abdul Rahman didn't leave me anything, apart from a mud house that shook when the thunder crashed and the rain poured. I lived off the kindness of other Muslims, either from charity or zakat. I washed the dead for God's sake, and always took whatever kindness or generosity the family of the deceased offered. One day, an hour before the afternoon prayer call, I heard a knock at the door. It was a bearded man, his beard full of gray hair. He spent quite a while asking God to preserve me and grant me a long life, before asking me to go with him to wash the corpse of a deceased woman. He said, by way of reassurance, that there was another woman with him in the car so it would be lawful for me to go with him. And anyway I was comfortable with the man. There was a look of goodness and faith in the features of his face. I quickly put on my abaya, picked up my equipment, and followed him into the street. I got into the back seat of a pickup truck, a Datsun or a Highlux, I can't remember. I sat next to a young woman who didn't return my greeting. She was completely wrapped in black and she simply made a gesture with her index finger as if she were saying 'la ilaha illa Allah' inaudibly and pointing to the heavens. The car set off and I uttered a blessing for the dead woman and asked God to have mercy on her soul. I asked God to grant them patience and consolation but I never heard the voice of the woman next to me at all. She never even said 'Amen.' Not a cry or a sob issued from her, and her body didn't shake with weeping. The driver, the old sheikh, was calm and composed. He drove very carefully, and never went too fast. When we had been going for quite a while I asked him, 'Is the place far?' At first he didn't answer but when I asked him for the third time he said, 'Put your trust in God, woman! We're almost there.' After that I stole a glance at the woman's feet. She was wearing cheap black plastic shoes, and her heel and the side of her leg that showed under the abaya almost glowed, they were so white. Then I noticed a gold ring with a zircon on her middle finger, and I felt convinced that she really was a woman. I had been wracked with fear that she was in fact a man in an abaya, and that the two of them had hatched some plot against me and were spiriting me out of the city. Even so, the man who was driving certainly didn't look like someone who would do such a thing. But then we're always hearing how criminals can mislead their victims by acquiring innocent, honest, and noble features. I was lost in these thoughts for some time, then I suddenly realized that we were heading down a steep hill to the west of the city, and that there was nothing around us save the hills and the highway heading to Taif. Then I noticed a black barrel of water tied in the back of the pickup, lunging left and right, and I realized that the situation was indeed very grave, and that my end may well be near. I tried to remain calm and not reveal my fear. I asked the woman next to me if the dead woman was her mother. She didn't answer and I said quickly, stammering with dread as I spoke, 'May God reward you handsomely,' as if it were my own funeral, and I was asking Him to have mercy on me and my life as my end rapidly approached.

"After a short while, during which we heard nothing but the hum of the car as it devoured the tarmac, I ventured to speak to her again: 'My daughter, say you take refuge in God from Satan!' but she didn't. She didn't say a word. I reached out my hand to touch hers, but the coldness of her palm made me jump, and the driver snarled, 'Shut up, woman! Take refuge from Satan yourself, and don't take my mind off the road.'

"I was silent, but my heart was not. It trembled like a hunted bird, chased by marksmen from tree to tree. It struck me that the woman might be dead and had just been propped up in the back seat, and this man was the killer. But then why did he want her washed and buried? A murderer doesn't care if he stuffs his victim in a rubbish bag and throws it into a cesspit or a well or any other place.

"Gradually the car slowed down, then turned onto a paved desert road. The yellow sun was now to the left of the car and we drove north. The driver never hesitated or slowed down to check the road in front of him. He clearly knew the way well, or was someone well-versed in the secrets of the desert, the hills, the wadis, and the dunes. Yes, for sure he knew the trees and the phases of the stars, and found his way by the lay of the land and the acacia and the shafallah and the rimth and ghada trees. A man like that would never lose his way, not even at night. The daughters of Na'sh, the stars of Ursa would lead him, and the Pleiades, and Canopus and Bellatrix, and the morning star that all true desert dwellers know.

"He drove the car between two huge mountains and approached a sand dune. I remember how surprised I was that there could be a sand dune there on such rocky ground. Anyway he stopped the car and opened the back door for the woman, who I'd assumed to be a corpse and would fall to the ground. But she got out slowly, calmly, obediently, and walked in front of him without closing the door. He walked behind her with deliberate steps as she headed with amazing posture and serenity toward the sand dune. Once they were on top of the dune he moved in front of her and she followed him down the other side. I saw their bodies gradually disappear until all I could see was the woman's head. Then that disappeared too without turning back once to look at me. It was as if she had made some resolute decision, or as if she were drugged and in a trance. She didn't say a word or interact with anything around her at all. My questions hadn't had any effect on her whatsoever.

"For a few quiet moments I sat alone in the car with the door open, then suddenly a gunshot shattered the silence of the mountains. Its echo reverberated for a long time. Even now years later I still hear the echo of gunshots in my little mud house and wake up terrified in the middle of the night. I don't know if there were three shots, one after the other, or if the echo bouncing round the mountains made it seem like the shots were repeated. At that moment the mountains wept openly, and my heart thumped wildly, as if it would fly out of my rib cage, and a shiver ran up my neck and made my hair stand on end. It was as if not a single drop of blood remained in my body.

"After a few minutes, which seemed like an eternity, I spotted somebody coming into view from behind the hill. It was him, plodding heavily along as if he were dragging his outrageous crime behind him, as if he were dragging a million murdered people. He untied the barrel of water from the back of the pickup. 'Get out!' he ordered me. I couldn't refuse, or speak, or even ask. I got out and walked behind him as he rolled the barrel along in front of him. He reminded me to bring my bag with my washing tackle— soap and oils and musk and ambergris and other things. I was just like the young woman had been minutes before: he walking in front and I following behind, stupefied and silent. I did not look back, just followed his huge feet as they sank into the sand and he lifted them out again with considerable strength and power.

"As I walked down the other side of the dune I saw her, spread out on the sand, still wearing her abaya. I began my work, taking particular care to mop up the blood that had flowed from her chest. When he reached the bottom of the dune he must have turned around and seen her silent and submissive eyes, waiting to go to eternal death. Then he shot her, the most important thing in his life. And now he was digging in the dust with the spade he had carried over his shoulder. He wept incessantly and wailed like a woman and his beard soaked up the copious tears. When the grave was finished we wrapped the young woman in her abaya and as he was placing her in the hole, he slipped and fell in on top of her. He began to howl inconsolably. I was afraid he might do something to himself so I began to ask God to have mercy on her soul and I said some prayers and consoled him. Then after it got dark he took me home."

Mother asked the corpse washer why he had done it, if he felt such remorse. The woman said she hadn't asked him until they were almost back in al-Atayef.

"A matter of honor," he said.

9

I t was dark, and the house was saturated with loss and absence and death. My brother Muhammad with his black beard seemed distracted and wore a grave expression on his face. All of a sudden he burst into tears right in front of me. I thought he had given free rein to his feelings for once, letting them run like wild horses through the open terrain of Grandmother memories. It was a startling departure from his cold and unfeeling self. But as mother calmed him down, he revealed that he was not crying for Grandmother at all. What had moved him was an overwhelming awareness of God's greatness, His wisdom and power, for does He not smite the sinners among His servants, even in this world, that they might serve as a warning to others among the living who go astray? He began to explain, reciting verses from the Quran and traditions of the Prophet before reminding us of the corpse washer's nephew, who had accompanied the men to the prayer and the burial. "Didn't you notice the long scar on his left cheek, on the entire left side of his face in fact, that looked like it had been made by a sharp knife or a sword that had fallen suddenly across his face?

"The first time I saw him," my brother said, "I felt as if I knew him from the mujahideen camp in Afghanistan. He reminded me of a Libyan called Abu Hurayra who taught us military exercises and how to use a kalashnikov the first couple of months I was there. He looked just like him if it weren't for that ugly scar on his left cheek. His beard was too light to conceal it and there was no hair growing in its

42

wake. So I thought I'd try to get to know him. He told me a remarkable story on the way to the cemetery. I can't get it out of my mind. It reflects the wisdom of the Lord so vividly. He told me about his mother and his aunt the corpse washer who washed Grandmother today.

"'My mother and aunt were both orphaned,' he said, 'when a huge truck took the lives of their parents, my grandparents. When my aunt, who was the youngest, regained consciousness in the wreckage of the overturned pickup truck my grandfather had been driving, she began to search for the corpses in the darkness until she and my mother were rescued by passersby, who took them to the nearest medical station, where they were treated for bruising. Despite the lucky escape, they would suffer for the rest of their lives.

"'They lived in my grandfather's old house in al-Atayef. They were years of hunger, cold, and poverty during which they were kept alive by the charity of kind Muslims. Then one day a neighbor advised them to learn corpse washing with her. There was good money to be made in it, she said, and a good reward in heaven too, and it was certainly better than the destitution of waiting for someone to knock on the door at night with a bit of money, or dreaming of a husband who would rescue them from the poverty and loneliness they were living in.

"'My mother and aunt bought rolls of white cloth from a clothing wholesaler in Souk al-Kabari. My mother would cut up the material into individual winding shrouds. That way she could justify to the families of the deceased the fee they were paying her in exchange for the washing and anointing, and the white shroud.

"'On one occasion, while my mother was washing the body of an old woman, the woman's daughter, upon learning that she was unmarried, prayed that her two noble hands would not see out the night save in the hands of a gentle-man who would protect and look after her. And it transpired indeed that she married that very night a man related to this family. He was an old sheikh and my mother was his third wife. They had scarcely been married a year when she gave birth to me one cold and cloudy night. My father closed his eyes for the last time the following dawn and I grew up with only my mother to take care of me. I never saw my father. It was as if this world would not tolerate my father and me to be together. I wailed in bewilderment as I experienced the world for the first time and he, weary of the world, croaked his last.

"'I had a desperate childhood, brother. What can I say? You did ask me about this wound on my left cheek. Anyway, my mother and my aunt continued to wash women's corpses and generally refrained from taking money despite our dire need of it. There were some people who insisted that my mother take her due after washing and anointing the corpse but there were others who didn't even offer her any money at all.

"'One Ramadan, when my mother had grown old, we set off—she, my aunt, and I—for Mecca. They both clung to my arm as I walked with them around the Kaaba and they repeated with me the prayer I was reading from a little leaflet that contained umra prayers. One thing distracted me from the prayer though, and that was the Meccan pigeons flapping their wings as they took off and then landed again among the other worshippers and pilgrims. Whenever we approached a gaggle of pigeons they would all fly away in a panic, escaping to the tops of the minarets, or up into the sky to disappear completely from sight. I thought there and then, why are the pigeons fly-ing away in such a panic as soon as we approach them while they are content to stay near everyone else? I remember that one landed quite happily on the shoulder of a man performing his prayers while a whole flock of them walked about calmly and unperturbed near another group of pilgrims.

"'At that time I could find no answer as to why the pigeons should be terrified of us, although I was able to explain it later. Anyway, after we got back, my mother was afflicted with a raging headache, so severe that she wanted to smash her head against the wall. She would have if we hadn't stopped her. We stuffed aspirin into her mouth, then Panadol, but the racket inside her skull wouldn't stop. After a few days she told me that when we had been walking around the Kaaba she couldn't actually see it. She could see me and my aunt and the other pilgrims doing their circumambulation, and she could hear our voices but she couldn't see the Kaaba, just a white space like the rest of the courtyard, cold white marble, and all those pilgrims circling around nothing. I presumed at that point that perhaps it was the headache that had caused her to lose her sight, but she confirmed that she could now see very well, and that in Mecca she had experienced no dizziness at all. The only thing was that she couldn't see anything where the Kaaba should have been.

"'I took her to a doctor and then to an eye specialist but we could find no physical cause in her head and her eyesight was sound apart from a slight cataract in her right eye. Apart from that everything in the head department was in good working order. A few days later, I called a sheikh and asked him about this phenomenon of not seeing the Kaaba. He asked me about my mother and about her work. I told him about the hard life she had endured and the tragedies she had suffered, and that she had borne all these tribulations with patience and had not complained. She had not been disobedient or fallen into temptation, I said, and she had washed the bodies of dead women, without, in most cases, receiving any fee in return.

"You are her son," he told me. "You must ask her exactly what she has done during her life."

"'I sat down with her one night. The pain in her head had receded, though she still wore a brown prayer scarf around it, tightly fastened. I asked her what she had done during her life, and that there must be some mistakes she had made. I tried to explain that every person might commit a sin or carry out a misdeed, but God is all forgiving and merciful to those who repent and believe. I still recall that I was leaning on her striped cushions, my eyes shifting from her face to the yellow light bulb dangling from the ceiling. As she confessed her crime, the light of the bulb suddenly dimmed and the world seemed to spin!'

"I asked the corpse washer's son if she had committed adultery. 'No, brother,' he said. 'She did worse than that. Imagine if you can. She was a witch. She put spells on people and hid the charms and talismans in the mouths of the corpses she was washing! She would stuff knotted hair and such like into dead women's mouths, stuff it with her finger right into the back of the corpse's wizened throat then close the mouth tight and wrap the shroud around the body. The magic would spread throughout the land and the poor victim would wander about sick and dizzy, going from doctor to Quran reciter to spell crafter but would never be cured unless the Lord wished for them to find peace. I was stunned. When I asked her, with stifled tears rattling in my throat, "Why?" she replied sadly that it had all begun when a woman tempted her with three thousand riyals. We could have lived for a whole month off that whereas charity and people's goodwill rarely exceeded two or three hundred riyals.'

"'What does all that have to do with the scar on your face?' I asked him. 'I'm coming to that,' he replied. 'Anyway, I didn't call the sheikh again, as I'd discovered the reason she couldn't see the Kaaba, and also linked it to the Meccan pigeons that shot, panic-stricken, into the sky whenever we approached them.

"'A few days later I sat sipping coffee in the sitting room when suddenly I heard my aunt scream. My mother had groaned, gulped noisily for air, and then expired. We found a doctor who confirmed the death and my aunt washed the body. I recall that the corpse was like a metal box; you know, when you tap your knuckle on a tank, that hollow sound you hear? Exactly! Her body was like an empty gallon can that had contained rancid butter, or an old barrel. If anything knocked against her the sound would echo disconcertingly in your ears. My aunt's hands washed gently, fearful of the loud clanging emitted by my mother's empty body. The fingers of her right hand were blackened too, as if they had just been taken out of the oven, especially the index finger. Perhaps it was that very finger that had pushed the little parcels of knotted hair into the corpses' mouths in order to bind other lives on this earth.

"'A friend and I set off with the shrouded body. We had decided to bury it in a cemetery on the outskirts of town after praying over it. The grave wasn't very deep: the bottom seemed quite close to us. But every time we tried, my friend and the gravedigger and I, to lower the body into the hole it would close up in our faces. Seriously! Just as I'm telling you. The grave would close up completely, as if there had never been a hole there at all, in that spot.

"'I decided to take the body back to our house in al-Atayef. It was dark when I got her inside and told my aunt. She wept until the source of her tears dried up. Then she thought for a while and said, "Get up, go and call him." I went out into al-Atayef Street, walked until I reached al-Khazan Street, then slipped like a stray feline into the telephone box by al-Futa Gardens. I took a yellow piece of lined paper with his number on it out of my top pocket. I heard his voice, mellow and reassuring. I described to him the grave closing up and my predicament with my mother's corpse. "Haven't you spoken to me before?" he asked with the insight typical of the sheikhs. "Yes," I replied. "I explained to you the problem of my mother, who couldn't see the Kaaba while she was walking around it with us, even though my aunt and I could both see it." Then I spoke frankly about how my mother used to cast spells and conceal magical charms inside corpses in exchange for lavish sums of money. The sheikh remonstrated with such vehemence that the saliva spraying from his mouth stung my eyes, and I held the receiver in my left hand as I wiped my smarting eyes with the back of my right. The gist of his diatribe was that if I had told him earlier perhaps we could have made her truly and sincerely repent before God and He would have forgiven her.

"'He told me that she could not be buried in a Muslim cemetery. He advised me to take her body into the desert, where I should select a large hollow and place the body in the center, just on the sand, and walk away immediately without turning back to look at it. He stressed this several times: "On no account, my son," he insisted, "should you turn back your head or body. Do not look behind you at all! Just leave the body and get out."

"'Imagine, brother, leaving your mother's body in the desert, and going home. Will I be leaving her to the birds of prey or wild animals? I asked myself. Would desert vultures swoop down out of the sky and pluck out her eyes? Would wolves and hyenas devour her? Would a mother wolf lead her cubs to my mother's corpse, tear the shroud to shreds with her incisors, and devour her face while the little ones consumed her breasts? But despite my misgivings I had no other

48

choice. I had to follow the sheikh's advice. I convinced my aunt, and she kissed her sister for the last time. I set off before the disc of the sun could cast its light on the faces of the low, shabby mud houses.

"'Eventually I came upon a swathe of uncluttered lowland completely devoid of hills or dunes or wadis or ravines. I took the shrouded body off the back of the small pickup and dragged it along for about ten meters onto a gentle mound of sand. I had been afraid to drive up to it in the truck in case the tires sank into the soft sand and I would expire of hunger and thirst in that vast desert without anyone coming to rescue me, unable to extricate the car from the devilish sand.'

"As the nephew of Grandmother's washer continued his mother's story at the front door—for he seemed unwilling to enter the house—his thumb snatched away a tear that slipped furtively from his eye. As he spoke, his eyes darted from one direction to the other and he did not look directly into my face.

"'What can I say? I placed the body on the cold, soft sand. It was the beginning of February and the sky was dark and overcast. I could see a huge black rain cloud in the west. I set off back to the car and went about seven steps before I stopped. The sheikh's advice was still ringing in my ears but I was like the woman in the old story who married the genie. He took her to live in his palace and allowed her to wander freely throughout it and go into all forty rooms except for the very last. He warned her sternly not to enter it but this made her curious and her heart became obsessed with the secret of the forbidden room. I was like that woman my mother had told me about so many times before I went to sleep on long winter nights.

"'I won't take much more of your time, brother. After seven steps more or less, I turned around to check on my mother's body laid out on the sand. At that very moment a violent thunderbolt shot out of the sky. One of its forks flew in my direction. It was only a small one but it seared the left side of my face,'—he stroked the scar—'and hot blood gushed out. I ran terrified, my heart thumping, to the pickup. I got in and started the engine, cutting through the torrential rain that lashed the road and hailstones the size of lemons that crashed down on the roof and hood.'"

The story had affected my brother deeply and he related it with deadly seriousness, stroking his thick black beard as he did so. "God's punishment is nigh," he intoned after Mother had gone upstairs and left us alone. I allowed no smile to show on my face, but inside I roared with laughter.

10

When he returned from Afghanistan in September 1986, Muhammad bin Hamad al-Sahi spoke incessantly about the war against the communists. He described the many miracles of the martyred mujahideen, from the scent of musk and ambergris over their graves to the signs that appeared mysteriously in the sky and on the ground warning of the enemy's presence. But while he spent the night tearfully recounting his adventures, his sister Munira waited impatiently to retire to her own private world in her room. For there, on the shelves of her little bookcase, a host of translated novels awaited her. She was not as eager for her brother's tales as she was to fill her young head, hair cut just below her shoulders, with the novels of Henry Miller and Isabel Allende. She would dab a hint of Miss Chanel on her breasts and hair, massage her earlobes with a few drops of scented oil, and imagine that her fantasy lover, Egyptian actor Hussein Fahmi, was lying on the bed by her side, reading with her line by line. Sometimes as he helped her turn the page, they would argue about who had finished first, and how she had to wait because she read more quickly than he did.

Hussein Fahmi found it an enormous pleasure to read with her. She imagined him reading the contours of her body, surveying each mountain and crevice, searching out its hidden treasures, as his clouds, heavy with hot rain, passed over her uncharted desert island and a ferocious heat seared her lips, as if they were ringed by a fire that longed to be quenched. Then *Tropic of Capricorn* would fall from her hands and she would slip into a dreamy sleep inhabited by butterflies with perfumed wings and the image of her lover as he carried her in his arms like Tarzan, protecting his woman from the wild beasts.

The photographs of the blood and fighting, the hunger and displacement, meant nothing to her. Nor did those ragtag Afghans as they carried their guns through the mountains. It was the characters of the Russian novels who were ever-present in her mind: mad Ivan, Dmitri the wronged killer, and the pure Alyosha. She would compare these heroes of Dostoyevsky's—who were nearer and dearer to her than anything else—to her own three brothers. She was so obsessed with the writer that she considered him a prophet. But the rambling novels and their immoral fantasies did not interest her brother Muhammad in the slightest. He was the middle brother, just two years older than she. His only world was there, with the guerrillas in the mountains.

In the final year at the al-Shafi'i High School, in the literature stream, Muhammad al-Sahi's eyes were vigilant, roving like the well-trained eyes of a hawk scouring the land for its prey. He had become obsessed with the anxiety and apathy filling the world, until one day the social science teacher, Zayd al-Khalid, picked him out. The teacher stroked his beard with his thick fingers as he looked at the uneasy young man and he began to pay more attention to him than to the rest of the students. Muhammad came first in class and the teacher presented him with a number of pamphlets urging jihad, and audiocassettes in which the mujahideen who had returned from Afghanistan wept as they described God's victory in the face of overwhelming odds against the tanks and fighter planes of the communists. Muhammad began to dream of an Islamic state and an Islamic government. Teacher Zayd al-Khalid took him on a trip into the desert near al-Hasy, a hundred and ten kilometers from the capital. There Muhammad attended lessons and listened to lectures asserting that the people in this sleepy little country on the edge of the continent were infidels who did not obey God's orders, who contravened His prohibitions and committed forbidden acts.

Muhammad's jihad began at home. As soon as he came in from school he would walk over to the television in a state of agitation and turn it off, while his sister Munira and his younger brother Saad were watching it. His mother didn't interfere but dealt with the matter calmly, turning it back on again once she was sure he had closed the door of his room. The father, Hamad al-Sahi, only came home to sleep and have his dinner, preferring to spend his time in his oriental perfume shop, whiling away the hours in search of a rare blend with which to seduce the rich and famous. As for Saleh, the eldest, he only rarely left the police academy and spent most of his time studying or with his friends.

Muhammad's character began to change. He became quarrelsome and malicious. He saw himself as a true upholder of the faith, eager to protect it from its enemies and those who did not strictly adhere to its divine rulings or were negligent of its basic principles, even if they were one's father, or mother, or siblings. So it was that one evening he took the vegetable knife from the kitchen drawer, cut the television cable, and threw the set in the rubbish skip out in the street. In so doing he wasn't just cutting through a wire, he was severing the last threads that bound his miserable and humiliated heart to his home and family. Perhaps it was this realization that made the distant father—who wasn't usually interested in anything except that elusive blend of perfume that would make his dreams come true—walk calmly up to his adolescent son, raise his hand into the air, and bring it crashing down onto the young man's cheek.

Muhammad gathered a few things and left. He roamed around for a while like a wild and solitary wolf, befriending no one, taking no company, until the soles of his cheap sandals alighted upon the hallowed ground of al-Madeena al-Munawwara. He wandered through the streets and alleyways, alone save for his sadness and apprehension and the bitter tears that no one saw. He entered the Prophet's Mosque many times to take a nap in one of its remoter corners or in the shadow of a column. As he slept he saw white birds leading him through green mountains. There were thorny trees scattered about that gave hardly any shade. Suddenly he saw huge gray birds dropping stones from their black beaks. He told himself they must be the airplanes of the enemy. And after the vagrancy and homelessness had taken their toll, a middle-aged man advised him to go to the village of Mahd al-Dhahab, more than two hundred kilometers away. It was a quiet place, and safe. There he would be able to find work in the gold mine.

11

He shared the small room with another worker called Salem Awad al-Yamani. They both received a pair of neatly fitting overalls, the kind you put your legs in first, then your arms, and zip up at the front, from the belly to the neck. They had to learn how to put them on. As for the boots, which were extremely heavy, it took a while to walk in them naturally without dragging them along the ground. Muhammad bin Hamad al-Sahi would never forget the first night. He stood in front of the mirror with the safety helmet on his head. The room was dark and when he turned on the lamp he reeled backward. "Hey, brother," his roommate teased, "Have you never seen a human car before?"

The workers got off the bus and walked in single file toward the rocky entrance to the mine where they gathered in a circle around the supervisor, Mr. David. He spoke to them in English, which was immediately translated into Arabic by the foreman, Ahmad Salimain. Everybody moved toward the wooden board that bore the numbers of the workers. Mr. David stood in front of the board and informed the workers that each of them should memorize his number. These numbers, he told them, were their new names. Muhammad al-Sahi's number was 37. He had to forget his name completely. Now he was brother 37. Likewise, his roommate, Salem Awad al-Yamani, would totally forget his name and become brother 12. Al-Yamani and al-Sahi would be consigned to hell and only numbers 12 and 37 would remain. Below each number on the wooden board was a nail from which hung a metal disk, one side of which was green and the other side red. With the help of the foreman, Mr. David explained that each worker had to turn the disk to the red side when he went into the mine. As soon as he came out again at the end of the shift he had to turn the disk to the green side so that the foreman could be sure that all the workers were out of the mine and no one was left inside.

A small engine towed the large carriage into the mouth of the mine and they disappeared like two wild rabbits slipping into their hole. As the workers walked through the safety zone, along the edge of the dark tunnel, the lamps on their helmets shone like stars in the dark, cavernous sky of the mine. Muhammad al-Sahi gazed in wonder at the twisting passages branching off in front of him, as if he were in a thick forest with many paths to follow and he had to choose his way. There were English symbols on the corners of the shafts and the ground was covered in mud. The digging machines gorged themselves incessantly on the rock spotted with little kernels of gold. While the humming of the engines lulled some of the workers to sleep, al-Sahi, number 37, picked up little stones that were scattered on the ground and held them in the light of his lamp. The gold hidden in the rock seemed to wink at him. It was the early morning shift on his first day and he was spellbound by the raw yellow metal glinting shyly in the folds of rock. He slung his pickaxe over his shoulder and set off walking. No one noticed number 37 as he silently slipped away into the terrifying labyrinths of the mine that wound and twisted under the rocky earth like a swarm of snakes, intertwining and separating again without rhyme or reason, just like the randomness of life itself.

At six in the evening the workers returned punctually to the gate of the mine and all turned their metal disks to the green side. Even number 12's metal disk was turned to green.

The board to the right of the entrance to the gold mine became a mass of green disks, except for number 37, which was still red. Ahmad Salimain, the foreman, began to check the numbers one by one but when he yelled out 37, no one answered. Then he asked the workers if anyone knew who number 37 was. His name is Muhammad al-Sahi, called out Salem Awad al-Yamani from the back. Ya Muhammad al-Sahi, shouted the foreman, ya Muhammad al-Sahi, but no one answered. The foreman informed Mr. David, who ordered a search and rescue team and a doctor into the mine with a small carriage and mobile floodlights. The red light shone off the rock walls like the light of an ambulance. After almost an hour they found number 37 wandering aimlessly as he looked for a way out. Every time he found a dark passage he said to himself, this is the one, it's bigger and wider than the others; but after following it for a while he would lose hope and turn back, choose another passage and set off again. In the end, all the tunnels and passages began to look the same, and in despair he sat down on the floor beside the track. Then he spotted the red light flickering in the distance, bouncing off the rock walls. He took off his helmet and began to wave its feeble light above his head until the search and rescue team found him. The doctor examined him and pronounced him to be in good shape.

Outside the mine, the workers stood waiting, distraught at the death of their new colleague. The saddest was number 12, for the two of them had spent the previous night joking and clowning about in the olive green overalls and the boots and the helmet with the lamp. Suddenly the men heard the sound of the search vehicle as it approached the entrance of the mine. They gathered eagerly on either side of the track, anxiously waiting for the rescue carriage to emerge. When they saw the olive green overalls swaying in the back of the vehicle they cried out in joy, "Welcome back!" until Mr. David yelled at them to shut up, and they fell silent.

Mr. David screamed into Muhammad al-Sahi's face, and swore at him in English for a while, then told him he'd have three days' wages docked for negligence and not sticking by his workmates. Al-Sahi betrayed no sign of emotion. He just stared at the foreigner and seemed not to understand. He may have still been terrified at the thought that he could have died in that dark crypt of a mine. What would it be like to die in a tomb of gold, he wondered. What would I do with all that gold as I lay there dying all alone and my breathing gradually fades? What am I doing here crawling along on my knees, dying a helpless and despicable death just to make a living, when I could die the death of a noble mujahid, over there in yonder mountains where martyrdom awaits?

He spent the night reading and had a game of pool in the recreation room with al-Yamani. He didn't particularly want to play but he felt it would be impolite to refuse. He thought about his mother and father and his sister Munira and his brother Saad. "I won't phone them. At least not yet," he said to himself as he contemplated his fresh young face in the mirror, his thin beard with the hair growing out in all directions, his mustache carefully trimmed, and his beautiful dark eyes. As soon as he clocked off the Thursday morning shift, he removed the overalls, boots, and helmet, showered and dressed, then hitched a lift with a truck to the main highway. There he caught the first bus to the Prophet's Mosque, where he spent the rest of the day and the following night in worship and contemplation.

After more than a month he came to understand the secrets of the mine and the teams working in it. He learned the warning signs that the explosives unit sprayed on the walls of the tunnels they were working in. Once when no one was looking he managed to snatch a can of the red spray paint. He disappeared with it to a deserted place and drew a caricature of Mr. David on the rock face. Then underneath it he wrote 'Davied' in poorly formed letters before running away with the can hidden in his clothes. On another occasion he slipped away from the two numbers he was collecting small rocks with and made his way to a quiet spot where he wrote 'Kill Davied,' and drew a pistol next to the words. The next time he passed the spot the writing on the rock had been sprayed out with the same color.

It was not, however, the vastness of the mine, the gold shining in its rocks, nor a life in the dark shafts and caverns that Muhammad bin Hamad al-Sahi was looking for. He dreamed of a life in the light, among high, rugged mountains. To this effect he had hung over his bed in the accommodation block a line of poetry copied out in his own hand.

He who fears to scale mountains shall forever live in low places.

He felt he was living in a pit deep in the bowels of the earth when he should be there in the mountains with the mujahideen, not scraping about in ignominy after a loaf of bread, with stupid Mr. David controlling his every move. So it was that one cold night he went outside and closed the door behind him. On the pavement outside the building that housed the workers' rooms he saw huge piles of locusts. He raised his head toward the spotlights and could make out the locusts dropping from the sky like rain. As he walked away, carrying the suitcase that contained his clothes, a few belongings, and the small amount of money he'd saved during the previous three months, he told himself that this place wasn't for someone like him. It was for locusts who have no greater goal in life than to eat and defecate. He was going to seek his dream in the struggle, and defeat the communists, or meet his Lord, may He be exalted and glorified, in the process.

He bought a plane ticket to Dubai and Peshawar then called home. The phone rang in his sad mother's house. Munira answered, her voice soft as an angel's, "Hel-looo!" He said hello and heard her down the line shouting, "Muhammad. Mother, it's Muhammad!" His mother almost fainted. He was just about to tell her that he was going to the jihad but suddenly he stopped. He told her he'd found a job up north, and that he was settled and things were going ok. He would probably come home for Eid, or at least he would call them. He didn't want anyone to come and look for him. Then he told her, "Forgive me, Mother, and pray for me, and tell Father I'm sorry."

12

I remember I put on foundation, lined my eyes with kohl, and filled in the lids with shadow. I carefully applied lip liner and filled in my luscious lips with dark ruby red lipstick. I was getting ready to receive my fiancé, Ali al-Dahhal, at home.

I squeezed my full, firm figure into a Fission stretch skirt that hugged my plump thighs and clung to my lower body so tightly I felt like a fish, or a mermaid to be precise, her bottom half a sea creature, her top half a siren.

I opened my wardrobe. I couldn't make up my mind which blouse to wear. All my new blouses were made of pure silk. After I started going out with my fiancé, I deliberately began to wear them without a bra, to entice his eyes and trap them like an insect in a spider's web.

It was a summer evening. Saddam Hussein had just announced that Kuwait was part of Iraq, and that the part had returned to the original whole. I was in my room upstairs, not sure what to do about the blouse. I decided to go for linen, for the summer in Riyadh is unbearably hot. We were like insects sizzling on a griddle.

I quickly pulled back my hair that was hanging over my shoulders and tied it up with a yellow scrunchy.

The bell rang flirtatiously. As soon as I heard it, I raced downstairs, my breasts bouncing about like two wild horses. But just as my hand reached the end of the wrought iron banister at the last marble stair, my brother Muhammad strolled in through the front door. I wasn't expecting him at that time and I never imagined it was he who'd rung the bell, especially as he always kept a house key in his pocket. Had he forgotten it? He stood in front of me bemused and asked me where I was going at such a late hour. I told him I was waiting for Ali. He frowned as he eyed me up and down, like a fisherman on the riverbank inspects the single fish he's caught to guess its weight and ascertain how much meat is on it.

"Are you going to meet him in those shameful clothes?" he said, trying to look composed.

"They're just normal clothes," I replied.

"No, no, no!" he shouted. "Go upstairs and change!"

After I had put on an embroidered caftan I felt sure that my brother would join us and sit with Ali, but much to my surprise he went out after welcoming my fiancé with a warm handshake. Unbelievable: even my religious brother was taken in by Ali al-Dahhal, and saw him to be a man of trust and reliability. Men! They have no idea, no intuition. But then what about me? How could all my senses have been so passive? All that was aroused, like a viper stirred from its slumber, were the tips of my fingers and the goosebumps on my skin as it surrendered to his trained and wondrous touch. He picked me up like a seashell discarded on the shore and plunged with me into the depths of the ocean. Water gushed inside me and engulfed me and I glowed with immaculate and resplendent light.

My mother seemed content to leave us alone together, and she never invaded our privacy. She thought that the marriage contract he'd signed was sufficient, even though we had not yet had our wedding night. Even my younger brother Saad, when I called him from work to tell him we'd be going to Maxime's Lebanese restaurant for lunch, confirmed he'd be joining us later but didn't show up. He thought that the mere possibility of his coming would be enough to stem the flood of kisses over the desert of my face or the running of lost fingers through the soft hills and valleys of my unexplored body.

I knew that Saad enjoyed his relationships. He was handsome and his heart was loathe to reject the plethora of soft fingers that knocked at its door. He was forever moving between girlfriends. He was a flirt and loved the attention. As for my brother Muhammad, he was busy with his company, which had opened branches all over the country. After he returned, disgruntled and disappointed, from the cold solitude of the mountains, he refused to work for the government. He believed that the government was corrupt and that working for it meant that one agreed with its corruption and godlessness. He was content to work with Father for a while in his shop, selling incense and perfume. Then he set up a small company with two of his secondary school mates with whom he'd gone on the desert trips. Initially the company was limited to small shops selling honey, all different kinds, from lotus honey to wild-flower honey. They imported it from the south, from Hadhramaut and Iran and from other places. Then they opened shops selling Islamic recordings, set up an Islamic publishing house, and established an office for Hajj and umra services.

My colleague Nabeela considered them con men and swindlers. That annoyed me and I retorted that she didn't like to see anyone being successful. She explained how they printed pamphlets containing concise advice on prayers and other religious matters. Then they approached philanthropists and asked them to pledge the cost of printing ten thousand copies of the pamphlet to be distributed free in mosques, schools, and shopping malls. But these unsuspecting patrons of charity didn't know what to do with all the pamphlets so the publishers undertake to distribute them, but they didn't distribute them. They sold them again to another do-gooder, and then a third time and a tenth time, and all the while the pamphlets were piled up in warehouses.

"They'll get what they deserve on judgment day," she said.

"But my brother isn't one of them," I protested.

She looked at me with a half-smile and a sarcastic look in her eyes. "You're too naive, just as I thought, always thinking the best of people," she declared before walking out of my office.

I didn't know if she was telling the truth, and those guys really were con men who took simple people like me for a ride, or if she thought I was naive because I hadn't let her sleep over at our house. She wanted to spend the night with me and she made no bones about it. "Your body's cute but it's fast asleep. You need someone to wake it up!"

Father stopped leaving the house after he was diagnosed with a mild thrombosis in the brain. When he came out of hospital he stayed in his room and didn't care if al-Dahhal or anyone else came around. He hated Ali's insensitivity, though. The thing that annoyed Father most was Ali's insistence on signing the marriage contract in the hospital, for Father believed that such business should be done at home, and that in the presence of my brothers it would have been more blessed and meaningful. But Ali was adamant. He wanted the papers signed quickly, even if it had to be done in the hospital. My father asked Ali to bring Sheikh Ibn Saleh— the local ma'dhun who officiated at the signing of wedding contracts in the quarter—and described his house, which was located near the main mosque. But Ali brought another ma'dhun whom my father didn't know, along with two witnesses. When the ma'dhun asked my father about the bride price, and my father fell silent for a moment, Ali blurted out,

"Sixty thousand!" Turning to my father, he added, "I'll bring it around to the house."

Was al-Dahhal, the imposter, so skilled at pulling the strings? Were you, my darling, a habitual thief, a seasoned criminal? Why did you show me all that love? Why did you allow me to become addicted to your love? I want so desperately to understand.

The Russian tanks that rumbled out of Basra heading for Kuwait had reasons and ambitions. What were your reasons for invading my heart with tanks of desire and snipers of passion urged on by Ibn al-Mulawwah, Kuthayr, and Nizar? Honey melted and juices flowed at your words of love, and nightingales floated through the sky above me free and unfettered as you recited those poems. You ate my voice in your mouth, chewed it disdainfully as you would a piece of gum, while my heart raced as if I were a sixteen-year-old girl. My thin lips were hooked on your prickly mustache but they could not quench their thirst on you, and I would spend the whole night consoling them as they recovered, trembling and exhausted.

13

Many birds had flown across my sky: lovers and admirers and those who stood besotted at the threshold of my amazing eyes, for everyone described them as such. All those mustachioed men who fell at my feet with noble aims, and dirty ones; all those obsessed with love and sex who swooned at my glances. But I loved you more than any of them. I loved your love for me, ya Ibn al-Dahhal, and that cultured persona you acted out so brilliantly, like all the other soap operas and scenarios unfolding in this strange country. Perhaps it was just that your performance was more brilliant and convincing than the others, and that's why I fell into your trap, for you didn't miss a single trick.

Until 13 July 1990 I was spending all my time between my job at the Young Women's Remand Center and studying for my master's degree, which at that point entailed compiling surveys to be distributed among the relevant university professors. I was assisted in this task by a number of undergraduate students in the sociology department at the university, who had been appointed by my Jordanian supervisor, Dr. Yasser Shaheen. One of these young men became a restless bird, flapping pathetically whenever he saw me. He wouldn't leave me alone, pursuing me with endless, and sometimes totally trivial, questions about the surveys. He would phone me at the Center and talk for ages. He continued to follow me even after he had handed in the surveys and in the end I was obliged to speak to him forcefully, "What do you want? Your job's finished. I'm grateful for what you've done and

you will be paid for cooperating with me and the supervisor."
Suddenly his voice changed and he sounded like a strangled
crow: "You're vain and selfish. You have no feelings. You
don't care about anyone but yourself."

Then he called me. "I love you," he said. "I can't get you
out of my mind. I think about you during lectures and I can't
concentrate on my studies." His voice trembled like a cat
about to breathe its last. I knew he was in the final year. I
explained that I wasn't suitable for him, that I was older than
he was, and that marriage didn't happen like that. He hung up
and I never saw him again. Some time later, his older brother
called me to explain how fond of me his brother was, then he
tried to chat me up as well. I didn't give him a chance. I didn't
want anything to do with either of them.

Unlike the two of them, my cousin Nasir was the same
age as me, although he certainly wasn't the kind of man I was
dreaming of. That isn't to say I wanted him to be like Hussein Fahmi, not at all, but I disliked the fact that he had relationships with lots of different girls at the same time. Even
most of our family knew about it. He'd broached the subject
of wanting to marry me with my eldest brother Saleh before
he traveled to Britain, but I'd refused. I didn't have any feelings toward him, not even embryonic ones, and could never
accept him as a husband.

I remember one night we were at their house on a family
visit. And because my elder sister Nura, who was married,
was Nasir's foster sister—having been breast-fed by Nasir's
mother when she was a baby—that meant that Nasir could
come right into the house without my sister having to cover
her face. He came in that evening and grabbed hold of me and
kissed me on both cheeks before I, utterly horrified, could push
him away. He apologized, claiming that he'd gotten us mixed
up because we looked alike. I think he spotted me alone in the

kitchen, saw his chance, and pounced stupidly. My mother and her sister were in the sitting room. They thought he had simply entered the kitchen unaware that I was there, but they did not know that he had insisted on embracing me in a most inappropriate way. Cousin Nasir continued to hound me right to the door of the National School when I worked there, and then the Remand Center. He'd pull up beside my car at the traffic lights and smile and blow me a kiss. Sometimes he'd even have the audacity to say to me, as I got out of the car, "I only followed you so I could wish you a lovely morning." He wouldn't take no for an answer and in the end I told my younger brother Saad, who was a close friend of his. They used to go out picking up girls together and they both had numerous relationships with women. When Saad heard what had happened they fell out and stopped seeing one another. Nasir never got in my way again after that.

Even though I experienced numerous advances, I was cruel and uncompromising in my responses. In fact, when I was little, I slapped one of the tribal elders. The men and boys had gathered for the annual majlis. It was at the time of Eid al-Fitr, at the end of Ramadan. I was eleven. I was wearing a pink satin dress patterned with ribbons and had a pink bag over my shoulder decorated with lace, full of sweets and presents the old people had given me. My big sister Nura had put blusher on my cheeks and pink lipstick on my lips. One of the men who was in his fifties—I didn't know them all when I was a child—noticed me and called me over. "Come here, sweetheart," he said, as he put his hand in his top pocket and took out his wallet as bait. He wanted me to think he was going to give me some money for the Eid, but no sooner was I, innocent little child all dressed up, standing in front of him than he grabbed my wrist adorned with bracelets and kissed me roughly on the cheek. I felt his rough mustache and saw white hairs mingling with the black. I managed to free myself from his grip and slapped him violently on the cheek, much to the delight of the other men, who burst into raucous laughter and applauded loudly. The man turned bright red with embarrassment.

It seemed as though I were carrying out my mother's advice. She had always warned me about men and I was taking vengeance on them all. Then al-Dahhal came along and wrought his revenge on me on all their behalf. He exacted the retribution all of them had ever wished to exact, making a mockery of me and my naiveté. An accomplished actor, he blew my mind like a desert storm blows away a solitary tree that has grown old and weak after many years of resistance. Oh yes, I had resisted everything, from roving hands and embraces to kisses, from frank flirtation to declarations of undying love.

My hand was quite capable of administering a direct and uncomplicated slap the minute anyone tried to kiss me, like the man in his fifties, or Nabeela, my colleague at work, or my cousin Nasir, not to mention all the others I had repelled with my calm, grave composure. And they withdrew in defeat, broken, mortally wounded. There were so many of them. In fact I was once the reason for driving a whole family from the old district of al-Marqab, where we lived when I was a child and where my body matured.

I was coming home from school one afternoon. The driver of the striped black-and-yellow bus dropped me off at the top of the street as usual, because it wasn't easy to take the huge vehicle down the narrow alleys of the quarter. I had only walked a few hurried nervous steps down the street, past the shop of Ali al-Yamani, when the son of our southern neighbor pounced on me and dragged me by the arm toward the door of their house. I screamed as I tried to free myself, and Ali al-Yamani came running down the street shouting, "Let the young lady go, you bastard! Let her go, may the genies paralyze you!" The boy ran off like an alley cat when he heard al-Yamani's threats, shot into their house, and slammed the rickety old iron door behind him. Al-Yamani panted for breath as he asked me if the boy had done anything to me. Seething with anger, I told him he hadn't, but inside me the fire of revenge was raging.

I reported the incident to my big brother Saleh as soon as he came home. He and my father went around to the boy's house, taking some of the senior neighbors and Ali al-Yamani as a witness with them. A few days later a large removal van pulled up outside their house and their cheap and tattered furniture was piled into the back: pots and pans and cupboards and carpets and curtains of many different colors. They left the district and never returned.

14

At home I was the neglected middle daughter. Not the eldest who, over time, becomes a surrogate mother and acquires double significance, nor the youngest, the last of the cluster, who wins everyone's affection, pampered by the family at home, spoiled by the relatives outside. I guess that's why I turned to books, to reading and research. I couldn't find emotional security. I felt ignored and forgotten by everyone at home, and was subjected to physical harassment by those outside. I never dreamed that I would hear anyone whispering softly, amorously in my ear, "My darling, my life!"

I couldn't believe my two little ears, whose still silence he would later scatter with his rapacious lips, when he said to me, "You are my world, my only refuge, my homeland!" Another night he whispered down the phone, "I feel that the whole world with all its pleasures and all its joys is gathered in your eyes." Never in all my thirty years had anyone been allowed to explore the recesses of my body and discover its hidden treasures. I never imagined I would find a man who would spend days extolling the beauty of my ears, or my amazing eyes, or speak endlessly about my ripe breasts, saying, "The whole world stands worthless and abased before your nipple." I felt as if Ibn al-Dahhal was creating me anew, but how I wish he never had and I had remained alone, my attention focused on my notes and my research on delinquent/criminal impulses in adolescent Saudi females.

A suppressed aggression had been growing inside me and it finally exploded with all its might in Ibn al-Dahhal's face when his secret was revealed. I struggled stubbornly, and with an unmatched determination, in order to rid my life of this fraudulent and deceitful creature. I resisted the arguments of the judge, Ibn Wasea, and I rejected outright his suggestion that I had fallen in love with the man who was standing there before me in court, and that he loved me even though he had changed his name. What have names got to do with it? Do we fall in love with names or people? What do we get married to, exactly? The judge asked that question. Damn him! How on earth could we begin a life together that was based on fraud and deceit? Who is going to treat the psychological wounds I have suffered? I don't trust anyone anymore. I am not sure about anything, not even myself.

I am a female. Just a female with clipped wings. That's how people see me in this country. A female with no power and no strength. My sole purpose is to receive, like the earth receives the rain and the sunlight and the plough. Supine and recumbent am I, unable to stand erect like a male. I submissively accept all things, even love. I didn't look for someone to love. I didn't have the right to do that in the first place. I was simply delighted when I found someone who loved me, and to be completely honest it wasn't loving someone that made me so happy, as much as it was being loved and desired. Isn't that an indication that I receive and accept and that I am simply passive woman, always the receiver, never independent? I belonged to my father in my childhood and adolescence, I will belong to my husband as a wife, then I will belong to my adolescent son, who will order me and forbid me, who will be my guardian and my trustee as long as I am alive.

When I was a child, my mother taught me to be wary of strangers, to keep to myself, to store my emotions and energy inside. It was my three brothers whose energies had the right to burst forth into the world. Even their genitals moved freely on the outside while mine were tucked inside.

You are female, they told me. You must display your femininity, lower your eyes, and cover your face with powders and creams like a clown to be noticed. My grandfather, who was a real misogynist, had a saying he always used to repeat, whether it was appropriate or not. It was a verse of folk poetry whose original author had long been forgotten: "Woman, you do up the bits on top for the sake of down below. You pierce your nostril all because of your ass." He used to draw out the last word with great relish.

A man likes his woman to smell sweet and look pretty, my mother said. He likes her to walk slowly, her steps sexy and seductive. You have to pay attention to your appearance, they told me, so the men will notice you. Damn them! I wish they'd all just get out of my way and go to hell, every last one of them.

For me to think and search and question, that meant I had begun to step outside, which was not what my mother wanted or what my father encouraged. He thought that if he submerged me in books as a child, I would not be curious to know about the outside world. He didn't realize that he was feeding an insatiable appetite. I devoured the pages but I did not venture out, remaining hidden until I eventually revealed myself through my column, "Rose in a Vase." My appearance to the outside world and the dissemination of my name was a curse on the family and the men of the tribe, but it did not stop me, and here I am, doing postgraduate research into the very shackles that bound me from the start.

I read a lot, and thought! And the more I thought the heavier I became. Even my buttocks gained weight. Imagine! I love the word buttocks. My mother desperately wanted my buttocks to be big and heavy and noticeable so I could show them off on special occasions and weddings, and as I moved between the mothers who were on the lookout for brides for their boys, they would notice my backside and gaze at it as it swayed firmly from side to side. What kind of God-forsaken world is it that judges people by their buttocks and behinds? Has the world come to look at a woman through her anus? Good Lord, forgive me. Mother, forgive me if you ever read this one day.

Mother, I realize you're always saying that woman was created from a crooked rib, and I know that the Prophet said woman is deficient in mind and religion. That is why I will try to be straight, strive to be perfect. I will reject the deficiency and replace it with perfection. Perhaps you'll say that these words I write are the epitome of crookedness, and that the only way for me to be straight is by keeping my feelings to myself. The more I focus inward the straighter I will be, and the more in demand with the men. But I don't want a man like our Nura's husband. She pretended to be stupid for him, humiliated herself so she could marry him and be at his beck and call every hour God sends. I don't want the man for whom my sister Mona cut and dyed her hair. How idiotic is that! She turned herself into a grotesque parody of Barbie. Does she think the man she wants to share her life with is looking for a blond bimbo? No way! I won't be like that. Ali al-Dahhal might well have caught me in his trap, and assumed the guise of a refined and respectable young man, even changing his name, his military rank, and his family, but he didn't make me pander to his male ego. He celebrated my femininity and adored me to the point of madness.

15

The way he treated me, you'd have thought my fiancé was a progressive, liberal kind of guy. Even so I was reluctant to reveal what I was really thinking because I sensed that deep down he had a village mentality. So I did not humor his liberal veneer by removing my face covering in front of the waiter in the restaurant. I would put my scarf around the lower part of my face and cover my nose and mouth. He didn't even notice, or perhaps he didn't understand, when an American soldier from the joint forces, standing with his companion at the door of Hardee's, complimented me. I had paid particular attention that day to my kohl and dark grey shadow, and as we walked past them toward the Cherokee the soldier noticed me and announced, "Beautiful eyes."

One time I was standing next to Ali at the display of sweets and chocolates in al-Malika Sweet Shop. Some distance away, a cocky young lad was staring at me quite openly. Ali noticed and moved to my other side to block my body and face from the boy's view. But the boy, who was wearing jeans and a short-sleeved shirt open at the neck, moved to the other side and edged a little closer. I felt uncomfortable and shot him a stern look. He sighed audibly when he saw my eyes and all Ali could do was take me gently by the arm and lead me outside. We quarreled. I blamed his lack of sophistication. He said it was my eyes that were to blame, and he apologized over and over again, assuring me that he loved me and that he would always be jealous. Then we left the busy traffic on al-Takhassusi Avenue behind and, driving down a side street, came into an upmarket area. It was deathly quiet and had escaped the fury of incoming rockets. He stopped the Cherokee under a huge sidr tree and began to devour my face in the darkness. I did not resist the desire of my lips and gladly yielded to his passionate onslaught.

I didn't hide anything from him, whether it was to do with my home or work life. I told him I'd volunteered to work with the committees that had been formed after the war broke out. Together with my colleagues Nabeela and Samya, I was helping to look after displaced Kuwaiti families. They were given temporary shelter at al-Malaz football stadium. I remember we had distributed blankets, quilts, and pillows and given fresh fruit to the women. But as we walked away we heard them muttering among themselves about us being downtrodden and oppressed, forbidden by law even to drive. I was already starting to get annoyed when one of the little girls blurted out, "Hey, Miss Brown Slippers!" I was wearing brown shoes, a brown linen blouse, and a beige skirt. I turned around and shouted back at her, "What do you want, you little refugee?" She leaped at me, spoiling for a fight, but a woman in her forties grabbed her. "You're the one who's a refugee in your own country," she yelled as she dragged the girl away. Her words riled us, and as we turned our backs to leave she rammed home the message, "You can't even drive your own car. Someone else has to drive it for you!"

A few days later a colleague who worked on the evening paper called me and invited me to join a demonstration. The participants were all educated women, some of them lecturers at the university, others civil servants, students, and journalists. They were planning to hold a peaceful procession and drive their cars along King Abdul Aziz Street, setting off from the intersection at the Salah al-Din Hotel and heading south in single file. Their objective was to draw attention to their demand to be allowed to drive. If ever a crisis hit like the one that had so suddenly befallen the Kuwaitis, with the surprise attack from their neighbor Iraq, how else were our women to rescue themselves and their children if their menfolk weren't around? That, my journalist friend explained to me, was the justification of their demand to drive their cars for themselves, instead of having Indian, Bangladeshi, and Indonesian drivers.

I was confident that if I sought my fiancé's advice about joining the women's driving protest, he would accept without reservation and perhaps even encourage me. On many previous occasions I had talked to him about women's rights and found him to be aware and sympathetic, to the extent that on the nights when he was away, I used to think how lucky I was to have found him. I had no idea where he went, by the way. Sometimes three, four, even five nights would pass without him calling me. When he showed up I'd ask him where he'd been. He'd tell me he was on official business that he couldn't disclose because it was part of his classified military work. I would say nothing, simply reassuring him that I appreciated the nature of his job.

After the scandal of the wedding night, I started to go back over his behavior, like a psychologist subjecting a laboratory rat to a series of experiments: where did the imposter, Mr. Ali al-Dahhal, disappear to for days on end? I came to the conclusion that he might have been in military detention due to the fact that he spent all his time with me, driving up and down the streets and avenues of the city. We associated every corner, each shop and sidewalk with a certain incident or song. Here's where I kissed you for the first time, and that's the supermarket where we listened to "You've Set My Heart on Fire." And at the Hala petrol station we shocked the petrol pump attendant in his red overalls as your hand disappeared into my skirt, which was hitched up around my thighs. He would spend entire days with me, our fingers intertwined as he gazed into my eyes and recited poems by Nizar. When I asked him about his work he'd say, "You are my work; you are my whole life."

Was my dear rat serving a prison sentence when he wasn't with me, or was he really checking in on half a dozen wild rabbits? For he did indeed have a home and children, and a mother and father, but they were outside the scope of the secret game whose strings he manipulated so perfectly with me, just as he concealed the fact that he was a mere private who had assumed the rank of major by playing a dangerous and clandestine role in this murky war. Now I wake up at dawn day after day, open the pink linen curtains with the large white flowers on them, slide back the aluminum frame, look into the street and ask, "Why did you do all that to me?" There is no response save the sad cooing of the pigeons as they warble despondently on the window ledge.

I had made up my mind to ask him what he thought about the demonstration, but my dear rat had embarked upon another ruse, a top secret mission, and I only saw him again after the driving ordeal was over and the mood in the country more akin to desolation.

16

S o, the matter between us and our enemy and adversary is not simply should a woman drive a car or should a woman not drive a car, though that may well be an issue worthy of debate. The matter is much greater than that. We are well aware of the simple intelligence that God, may He be adored and glorified, has given to us. We know what lies over the brow of the hill. This demonstration is the visible face of a whole host of other insincere activity. Let us not beat about the bush. Let us speak openly. For this unholy display has been preceded by articles in the press and the scientific and literary reports that I have referred to. There have been recorded lectures, some of which I've heard, talking about women's liberation. Women's societies here and there have been conducting secret activities, taking numerous tours to the provinces, gathering supporters and helpers, writing books, and conducting quiet propagation among the ranks of women. Many other serious incidents will follow this one if society does not move in the correct way, does not strike with an iron fist each saboteur and wrecker, whatever his color or appearance, his personality or position in society. They are the vanguard of a mighty army. They are waiting over the brow of the hill. Other regions might move, and those who did what they did may devote all their efforts to doing more, and repeat the attempt. Incidents of young women driving cars might engender something much more serious. All of these things can surely happen, and much more can happen, because this

*is a bold step or, as some have said, it is a shift in the mind-
set. When, in the future, they wish to chronicle the women's
liberation movement in the Kingdom, people will talk about
the protest that took place one Tuesday evening in AH 1411 as
a shift in the mindset, a sincere and courageous stance. God
alone knows if true believers will censure and disapprove of
it, and talk of the instigators who tried to drag society into
depravity but failed. Others will talk about it in their own
way. No doubt the external enemy will be delighted and will
support this kind of movement in order to subvert the Islamic
sensibilities in our country.*

My brother was sitting in the living room listening to
the voice of the preacher booming out of the tape player. He
stroked his thick beard and looked at me through his glasses
as I came downstairs on my way to the kitchen. He beckoned
me over. I walked up to him as he sat there on the sofa, having
forgotten to take off his shoes, and he told me to sit down.

"Where are you going?"

"To make tea."

"Later."

*Public denunciation means that each one of us must do
something. Every one—man, woman, young, old, educated,
ignorant, student, teacher—must do something, anything;
write a letter, send a telegram, a tape, phone up, visit offi-
cials and religious scholars, speak to these women per-
sonally and advise them, at their places of work and in
their homes, wherever they are, so that these women and
whoever is behind them will realize the extent of society's
concern. Society could be boiling with anger while these
women sleep soundly, imagining that the issue has passed
peacefully and without incident. That is why their guardians
should be advised, and reminded of God, may He be adored
and glorified, and alerted to the scandalous nature of what*

80

*is happening, and encouraged to take control of their inso-
lent and foolish daughters . . . .*

"Who's that?"

"A sheikh."

"I know that. What's he so worked up about?" I said
coldly.

"We are not as foolish as you think."

"Who are *we*?"

"The cassette. It's the title of the cassette."

*We must widen the scope of our denunciation to cover all
the previous incidents that we were silent about in the past,
and we must reveal the role of the secularists, and their hidden fingers, in our country. We must expose them and speak
about their plots, and monitor what they publish in the press
and broadcast on the radio and the television. We must do
this for the sake of all Muslims so that what is hidden may
be seen.*

"It's a nice title."

"It's nicer that he's exposing those secularists in the press,"
said my brother with an accusing look in his eye. Then he
uttered God's name, reached over the back of the sofa, took a
copy of the cassette out of a little bag and handed it to me.

"Just in case one of your colleagues was with those
whores."

"Who?"

"The car women!"

"No!"

17

Back in my room I turned off the three ceiling lights and turned on the bedside lamp. I pressed the eject button on the stereo and replaced the Muhammad Abdu cassette with "We are not as foolish as you think." It could be the title of a novel, I thought to myself, or an interesting article in the paper. I lay on my back and listened.

An intelligent pamphlet, but its purpose is exposed because it is originally a letter written to a senior official; and its intended destination was to reach his office, but it would seem that the letter lost its way and ended up being distributed on the streets. This letter is well-known, but if it had reached the official to whom it was written, would it have been distributed in public? Then ask yourself if there is anything in what those women did to justify its distribution? That's one point. The second point is that the pamphlet begins by talking about women having been granted permission to volunteer for nursing, and thanking the authorities for that. This proves that these people don't know when to stop. It's a question of escalation: take and demand more. After they're allowed to do nursing, and the door is opened wide to them, and they see they've made tangible progress in what they covet, they aren't satisfied. They don't say, "Let's wait a year or six months." No. Immediately they started this movement, which reveals the existence of a ravenous greed in their souls. That's why leaving the way open for them to volunteer will only lead to . . . .

The flame of the candle I'd placed on the square coffee table flickered with fear, even though the window was closed and there was no draft coming in. I saw the huge shadow of the flower next to it dance on the ceiling above me, while the preacher's voice filled the four corners of the room.

The pamphlet says, and I quote: the society that has given us women so much is calling us to return the favor, and for all of us, whatever our class and background, to offer it our loyalty. I would like to ask these women, what have you given to society? You haven't given a thing to society. Is bringing in wretched western values a service to society? Is distracting the whole of society with an issue that is of no use to anybody a service to society? Is confronting the finest and most decent body of men in the Islamic Nation a service to society? A fourth point. The demand we have spoken about is for a woman to drive a car in the city of Riyadh. Do you know why inside the city? Because it is not permissible for a woman to travel without a mahram, so the driving must be within the city limits. That's why they put forth the reasons. What are the reasons? One, the presence of a foreign man inside the house, and the necessary presence of a woman alone with him, on occasion, inside the car. Masha'Allah, God bless them. These women say that by driving a car themselves they will not contravene this religious interdiction. I consider this an insult to our intelligence. We as a society have made the presence of the driver necessary, then we search for a cure and a way out of this necessity. In other words, we treat the patient by cutting off his head. The strange thing was that some of them wore the burka, even though wearing the burka was never a recognized convention.

The shadow of the flower fluttered nervously on the ceiling, and the ceiling looked as though it were about to cave in. I couldn't get rid of that childhood fixation, staring at the ceiling that was moving nearer and nearer the harder I looked at it. I felt if I stretched out my hand I could touch it, but when I did I couldn't, even though it seemed to hover just above my chest:

The second reason for their demand is the cost. The women say that having a driver is a financial burden. We'll dismiss the driver and we'll take his place. When they took the cars they said to the drivers, "Go, go! We do not need you after today. Poor things they are. They came back embarrassed, still needing their drivers. These financial burdens are a strange pretext. Every home has ten servants, opulence and extravagance, ornaments and furniture, and they're only talking about the financial burden and avoiding prodigality and preserving the nation's economy in this one area. The third reason is that a lot of immoral things are happening inside homes as a result of the driver and the maid inside the home. I say it looks like the pamphlet wants these immoral things to happen inside the home and outside it too.

The candle flame died suddenly, I don't know why, and the shadow on the ceiling disappeared. I was alone in the darkness and the voice of the preacher still filled the room.

The fourth reason is that during times of crisis and emergency women take the place of men in protecting the home front. That's how they put it—protecting the home front. This needs something far bigger than a woman driving a car. If this is what their intention is, then perhaps they have revealed something they would rather not have revealed, because I don't believe that protecting the home front is limited to a woman driving a car. By saying that women protect the home front they're simply concealing their desire for her to undergo weapons training. These women want to be soldiers, they want to be men, but to still wear a beautiful, enticing dress instead of a man's thobe. The last point with reference to the pamphlet is that it exploits religion, for the pamphlet is written in a religious style and tone. Now, why is that?

As he asked the question why, my hands were flapping about in the darkness trying to find the off button on top of the tape player. As soon as my finger touched the button there was silence. The scent of jasmine from the candle that had gone out moments before filled the air. I slid under the sheet and my mind stumbled along behind a host of difficult and disturbing questions.

18

I n the stillness of the desert city, as the cool sun dips lazily toward the unknown horizon, people are deep in their afternoon slumber, having filled their stomachs with long-grain American basmati rice, followed by cups of cheap milk. The sports pages have fallen across faces bloated with sleep as their bodies lie stretched out on their beds, having checked the gas masks in case of a chemical attack. Everything is silent, deep in siesta, as forty-seven women gather at al-Tamimi Shopping Center. They ask their Pakistani, Indian, Bangladeshi, and Indonesian drivers to get out of the cars and they take their places behind the wheel. The drivers gaze at one another in amazement, exchange questioning looks, then begin to talk together animatedly in languages that sound like birds chattering.

There are thirteen cars, driven by thirteen women. In each one there is a passenger or two or more. They set off slowly in single file toward the traffic lights, then turn right and continue until the next lights, where they turn around and head back. At that point they are spotted by a bearded man in his forties. He opens the window of his battered old Datsun and shakes an angry fist at them, but the women pay him no attention and carry on until the first lights. As the lights turn green a man steps out in front of the line of cars. He seems to want to flirt with them, and won't move out of the way, but then two young men come, stand next to him, and tell him off, and he, thinking they are security agents or some kind of military, shoots off in alarm, leaving the way open for the motorcade. At the next lights the first-ever procession of cars driven by women in this desert city comes to a halt when a traffic policeman, who has just turned out of Aruba Street, signals to them to stop. A university professor winds down the window of her Chevrolet to speak to him. She is wearing a niqab, and all that is visible of her face are two nervous eyes. Clearly shaken, the policeman looks at her and asks her for her driving license. She takes out an international driving license she obtained when she was studying in America. He looks carefully at her photograph on the license and then back at her eyes. Then he goes to the next car, looks at the driver's license for a moment, and stares into the driver's eyes for a long time. He repeats the procedure with the rest of the cars. He has no idea what to do. The women are driving well; they are dressed modestly, and they haven't broken any traffic regulations. He asks the women to pull over into the service road and begins to contact his superiors.

Suddenly three GMCs turn up and a group of bearded men, wearing short thobes half way up their calves, get out. One of them comes over and bangs his fist on the hood of the Chevrolet. As he bangs, he curses violently and waves his hand at the university professor. Passersby start to gather on the pavement, and the police car parks. An argument ensues about who is responsible for these delinquent women. The traffic police see it as a traffic violation that concerns them alone, while the men of the Commission for the Promotion of Virtue and Prevention of Vice believe that it is a religious and moral infraction that is their business and no one else's. In the end they agree that a traffic policeman and a member of the Commission should ride in each car full of women, one to drive the car to the police station and the other to act as mahram for the women.

Later that same night the women came out of the police station. Each had brought a male guarantor to make a formal pledge that his wife or his sister or his mother will never commit such an offense again. The university professor thought that they would be welcomed as heroes at the university but sarcastic comments and defamatory accusations were stuck on her office door. Inside the lecture hall, she found written on the board: "The secularist rejects religion and God's rulings." As soon as she entered most of the students walked out in silent protest at what she had done. A few days later there appeared in mosques and universities, schools and government offices, and in the streets, a paper containing the names of the women who had "called for wantonness and abomination." These scraps of paper flew around the city like deranged birds. All the while Munira al-Sahi was calling her journalist friend to check if she was all right. Eventually she discovered that the woman had been sacked from the newspaper and confined to her home, where she was counting the walls one by one. She had decided to do the room a different color and had gone from journalist to decorator, learning how to put plaster and paint on the cement walls. She was venting her fury on her room, as if she were repainting her soul. Lots of people in this city used to keep their thoughts to themselves but the drums of war have brought some of them out of their silence.

Munira wondered what the reaction of her family and fiancé, Ali al-Dahhal, would have been if she had taken part and driven her car down the street. Every time she was tempted to think she had escaped the scandal and the public naming, she took out the piece of paper from under her feather pillow and looked at the names:

The names of the wanton women who are calling for depravity and corruption on the Earth:
1. Aysha bint Ayyash – University professor – American infidel

As Munira al-Sahi imagined her name listed proudly with the names of the other women, she began to ponder what the reactions of the people around her might have been. Her father would have succumbed to the brain tumor and passed away months, even years, before his time. Her brother Muhammad would be furious with the incessant ringing of the phone, and quake with anger as he stroked his beard. He would spit in her face every time he received a call from someone offering advice or admonition. As for her sister Nura, her husband would forbid her from going to visit the family home "as long as your whore of a sister is in the house. She could ruin my daughters with her depraved ideas." Meanwhile her younger sister, who danced incessantly and listened to the songs of Muhammad Abdu and Abdul Majeed Abdullah, would change, or would be obliged to change, into a religious woman, in order not to remain a spinster. She would have to don an ample abaya and stockings and black gloves. She would turn into a black angel. Perhaps her older brother, Major Saleh, would be proud over there in Britain as he confirmed to his English colleagues that his sister was politically aware, courageously demanding her rights, and subjected to all kinds of pressure for the stance she was taking. But the minute he got home, he'd take off his military belt and beat her around the head with it, in the hope that the remaining seed inside her brain that had not been ground down would be crushed to smithereens, and that her pride—how many books had she read?—would be torn to shreds, just like her face that would bear the marks of his attack. As for the mother, she alone would embrace her errant daughter and blame herself most of all for marginalizing her middle girl and ignoring her, which is what made her seek attention and do anything to make others notice her.

Perhaps there would remain only one who still cared for her, who would not blame her at all for the religious crime she had committed—for that's what they have all called it. Only one would become closer to her during these difficult days, cuddle up to her, and sleep gently in her arms: her friend Susu, the affectionate Siamese cat, who would be overjoyed to have her dearest Munira back with her after having been abandoned in favor of Ali al-Dahhal. Yes, he too would be distant and withdrawn after seeing his fiancée's name broadcast all over the city. He would evade her, escaping like a dream on a summer night, ignoring her repeated calls as she tried to contact him, desperate to explain the situation.

Munira was relieved that she'd escaped the ordeal unscathed. The results would have been too terrible to contemplate. When she reviewed her knowledge of life, she realized she did know how to attack and withdraw at the right time, how to demand her rights, and how to forego them if the need required. She had fought in order to remain a famous and controversial journalist, standing up to the men of the tribe, and she was able to put up with the strict supervision under which she left and entered the house. She would do what she wanted without need for conflict with any of them.

She stood for a long time in front of the mirror, feeling deep gratitude for her wide eyes—her unexpected trap for passing men, stronger and more deadly than the spider's web on the ceiling of her room. But then, aren't flies more intelligent prey than men? For flies have the ability to sense through their antenna, which helps them to avoid the trap at the last moment, while men just ran panting after her marvelous eyes—dreaming that they might obtain some momentary physical pleasure from her body—and fell head-long into the trap. Then she spat them out like date pits.

Did Ali al-Dahhal come to take revenge for what I did to the men before him? she asked herself. She thought that she would rail against him as a wind uproots a sturdy tree if ever he showed he did not take her feelings seriously. She never thought for a single moment that he was plotting her demise and a scandal that would many times outweigh a peaceful procession and the natural rights of women who dream of driving their cars in the desert. Later she was to think that per-haps if she had joined the women, and been suspended from her job for three years, and endured her family's ire at the dis-grace she had brought upon them, it would have been easier to bear than the scandal of that night. Munira al-Sahi began to look back over the seemingly insignificant occurrences of her time with al-Dahhal in the hope that they might help her, a woman not entirely lacking in intelligence, to piece together the hidden personality of this dangerous character.

19

My brother Muhammad came in and sat with us. As usual he had brought something new with him, and he walked over to my father and pulled a piece of paper out of his pocket and began to read:

There has been lots of talk about women driving cars. It is well-known that this will lead to immoral and licentious acts, of which those who call for it are not unaware, among them the possibility of a woman going out on her own, which is forbidden by the Faith. Such situations lead to the public display of women's faces, and mixing with men without restriction or limitation, and the committing of unlawful acts, for which reason these matters are haram. The immaculate and unsullied Revelation has forbidden all means that lead to unholy and irreligious conduct, considering them to be haram. God, may He be glorified and exalted, has commanded the wives of the Prophet and the wives of the believers to remain in their homes and to be veiled and to refrain from exhibiting their beauty and charms to those men who are not mahram, because this leads to promiscuity, and promiscuity will bring about the ruination of society.

My brother spoke loudly so that he might allow us all to hear the new fatwa. I felt as though he were directing his imposing voice and his searing glare toward me. I was sitting at the other end of the room, where I had spread out some of the surveys that had been filled in for my research. I was preparing the results myself after my Jordanian supervisor, Yasser Shaheen, had been deported and my project, which I had loved and dedicated so much time to, had been suspended.

"Is that from the Mufti?" asked my father.

"Yes."

"May God preserve Islam for us," commented my mother as she pulled herself slowly to her feet and took away the tea and coffee cups. I was thinking about the fatwa, and remaining in the home, and what is forbidden and what is unlawful, and beauty and war and America and jihad, and women volunteering to join the nursing patrols because of the war, and the young men joining up, and all the pamphlets in the streets, and the clamor of audiocassettes in the souk, and Ali al-Dahhal, who had appeared with the war, and Desert Storm, and the daily report on the conflict, and occupied Kuwait, and the divisions in the Arab World, and the calls for a joint Arab force, and Egypt and Syria and the Gulf States.

I was wondering how a tender bottle, with mysterious Indian symbols on its surface, was supposed to deal with all these things going on in the world. Am I to write about all this? Isn't my fiancé Ali al-Dahhal part of this war? Isn't love also war in one way or another?

I was always asking questions but the noise of war and battle—the loudest noise of all—would always drown them out. Whenever I asked him where he'd been, al-Dahhal would exploit the circumstances of the war and say, "I was on a secret mission." Then he would add, and he really knew how to scare me, "You're being watched," because I was his fiancée and he was in a sensitive position. I wasn't supposed to ask any questions. To hell with the secret mission you've made up, ya Ibn al-Dahhal. Isn't your secret mission to destroy me in order to avenge your honor? Is your national duty to destroy a woman whose only fault is to be the sister of someone who insulted you? Was it you who started the great war in the Gulf so that you could wage your small war with me? I don't understand very much anymore in the face of all this terrifying confusion.

20

The first strikes against Baghdad were surgical, according to the media. The live broadcast of the bombardments looked like a children's video game. We were all terrified that poison gas would come into our homes. Fear swelled in our throats every time the media showed the clips of the gas attacks on the Kurds in Halabja. The images of the bodies covered in flies had us believing we'd all drop dead like stunned insects if it weren't for the tape we'd stuck around our windows to save us.

My father stared emptily at the TV screen while Muhammad read reports of a conference the university had held entitled "The Sacred Jihad." It had been attended by the ulama and other Islamic thinkers. "Hypocrites!" my brother called them.

"The wind of Paradise is blowing . . . . Where are you who desire it?" sang Muhammad Abdu on the stereo in the living room. Muhammad leaped to his feet and went to turn off the music. "What Paradise, what jihad?" he boomed, his voice loud and hoarse like a raging camel. "There is a huge difference," he expounded, "between using the evildoers to smite the evildoers and thinking that a battle led by the Americans is a jihad that will lead us to Paradise."

He was addressing Father, whose head had slumped back against the cushion. He had started to snore, softly at first but with ever-increasing volume, until Mother came to wake him so that he could go up to his room.

Father did not utter his ubiquitous response, "The sheikhs know best," in front of my seething and rebellious brother, but he said it to the rest of us—Mona, Saad, and me—without a second thought. And whenever he was alone with my mother, he would elaborate at his leisure, "God preserve them for us," he would say as he reeled off the blessings and bounty that we'd experienced in our lifetimes. Then he would finish his words with the old adage, "Two blessings never appreciated: a body sound and healthy, a country safe and wealthy." Mother, enchanted by his way of saying things, would hand him his cup of coffee.

I love my father. He is my only refuge and consolation. I feel that the faint traces of the smallpox on his face and around his eyes have led him to see the world differently, and even if Muhammad's words or Saad's behavior didn't please him, he rarely scolded them. Instead he would resolve the matter with a long sigh accompanied by the phrase, "God preserve us."

21

On a smooth silk sheet I reclined my exhausted body. The war had ended—my war with al-Dahhal and society, its commissions, its courts of law and its men; and the Gulf War, which left behind only the dead buried in mass graves and huge plumes of black smoke rising skyward from Kuwait's oil wells. Saddam had tossed a final matchstick and sat there for a while, contemplating the dark billowing columns that hovered ominously over the land like genies who did not say, "Your wish is my command." Then Saddam and his soldiers took their leave. Meanwhile Ali al-Dahhal had walked out of my life after throwing his last matchstick into the lake of my heart and dark clouds of malice toward all the men in the world issued forth.

One evening, before the land war broke out, Ali al-Dahhal had stopped at the gate of the Young Women's Remand Center and called me from the guard's telephone to ask me to go out with him. I remember I was studying the case of a new girl in the Center who had been assaulted by girls older than her. I had just begun to get to the bottom of the dilemma, and understand the way the nurse had exacerbated the conflict, when the phone call came. I closed the file and put it back in the cabinet that held the social and psychological cases. I opened my small silver embroidered handbag and took out the compact mirror and brown lipstick to do my lips. As I hurried out of the building the case of the young girl was still preying on my mind.

I went out through the huge iron gate and there he was in a white thobe talking to the guard. He wasn't in the usual white Jeep Cherokee, though I no longer paid much attention to his various cars, most of which he acquired from car rental firms. He always chose top-of-the-range cars, in order to give me the impression he came from a well-to-do background. That's why this time, just as on previous occasions, I didn't look too closely at the car he was in. If I had looked at it from the outside, even for a second, I would have realized that it belonged to my brother, Major Saleh, the dark blue Caprice that I knew so well. He'd left it in the office garage when he was sent with a delegation to Britain to do a training course. If I'd thought for a moment about the plastic bird that hung from the rearview mirror, I would have remembered my brother's little girl who had bought the bird when they were on holiday in Malaysia as a gift for her father, specifically so that he could hang it on the mirror.

Why didn't I notice the signs? Wasn't the good Lord sending me numerous signals to wake me from my slumber, to rouse me from the stupor of my love for that man? Or is it that women don't see anything once they fall in love? Did I love him for who he was or simply because he loved me? I was always going over the odd events, those glaring discrepancies in the watertight script al-Dahhal had crafted. And despite that, I did not wise up to them. I was a blind, besotted creature led on by the stick of her emotions, the stick that twists and distorts facts and drives her on through the fantasy like a contented stray sheep. If only my father or my brother had taken the stick and beaten some sense into me.

The funniest thing was that al-Dahhal stopped the car for several minutes outside the Italian Coffee Shop on Tahliya Street and got out to buy two espressos and two bars of chocolate. And even though I put my cup next to his in the cup carrier I still didn't notice that it was the exact same place I had put the glass of mixed juice my brother Saleh had bought me from Mama Nura's juice bar when he had picked me up from university one day. How come I didn't make the connection between the two cars, or at least become suspicious? Was it because, when I put the cup of coffee down, I was too busy talking to him about the case of the young girl who had been assaulted to pay attention to the inside of the car?

And when he popped a tape into the stereo and the mellow voice of Muhammad Abdu flowed out: "If you kept your word and came one day to see me," I suddenly interrupted myself in mid-sentence and gasped:

"Allaaah . . . just imagine?"

"What?" he asked.

"My brother Saleh really loves this song. I remember driving down Green Belt Avenue as he sang along, "If your heart is true I'll love you even more."

My soft voice, which al-Dahhal was so enamored of, sang the words. He said it was like drops of crystal cascading over marble tiles. I sang along, "If you would allow me your lips and some time, I'll be sated and I'll sate the rose of your mouth."

"To be honest," he told me as I, in my lover's trance, continued to sing, "I'm a touch jealous of your brother Saleh. I'd like to meet him." Damn your genius, ya Ibn al-Dahhal. How confidently he spoke about my brother, like someone who didn't know him at all, who had never seen him. Yet it was he, a private in the mail corps, who had spent his life standing at my brother's office door like a mongrel, floppy ears dangling, ready to spring into action whenever the phone rang, or my brother's voice on the speaker shouted, "Private!" and up he would jump in alarm, panting like a pooch. How did he burst so confidently into my secluded kingdom on the night of 13 July 1990—that's three days after my brother left—ready to set about his games of manipulation? He entered the very heart of our home, from the men's majlis to my own room. Previously, when my brother had sent him with the newspapers, he would stand at the gate and humbly hand the papers and magazines to the Filipina maid Lillian before slinking away.

All things conspired in his favor. Even Lillian's tongue was tied and did not betray him. She confided to me after the scandal broke that she knew he was the same person who sometimes brought the newspapers and magazines from my brother's office, but she thought that we knew that too. To her mind there was nothing to prevent him from proposing to me, and in any case she knew not to bring up a matter that was none of her business—for it was basic good manners that she did not discuss her employer's affairs. Thus Lillian witnessed the deceit but did not speak.

The events of my private war inside the house greatly resembled those in the war outside. Every member of the household was surrounded by signs of deceit and duplicity but no one could see the situation for what it was. It was the same with the real war grinding away to the north, just like *Star Wars*. It was broadcast live on TV every night, and yet no one saw the duplicity and deceit that lay behind it, or the conspiracies and machinations that were concocted as it raged, just as no one detected the conspiracies and machinations hatched by Ibn al-Dahhal as he put the whole of the human race at his service. Even fate itself conspired on his behalf.

Whenever we sat in the coffee shop drinking Turkish coffee and cappuccino, his walkie-talkie would be crackling all the time with numbers and code words. Sometimes he'd be addressed directly, "Major Ali!" and he'd respond and issue orders. A remarkable creature, undeniably brilliant at performing the role. He never forgot or said a wrong word; not even the color of his face changed.

I'll never forget how the waiter at Maxime's knocked on the wooden screen surrounding us. "Major Ali. There's a telephone call for you." I was stunned. How did the waiter know his name? How did the caller know he was there, in that restaurant and at that particular time? When he came back he told me that the waiter knew his name because he had heard it on the walkie-talkie. The caller was from his department. It was an emergency and we had to leave immediately without finishing our coffee. He didn't even take the change from the fifty-riyal note he'd given the waiter.

He often tried to impress upon me the importance of his role in the war. He even had me convinced I was being watched and followed, because of my connection with an important person like himself. God damn you, private! So much talent and all you do with it is wage a small war on me.

22

He rang me one evening at sunset. He told me he was leaving the following day on a mission to rescue an important person who was missing in Kuwait. "Pray that I return safely to your eyes!" he whispered melodramatically. I cried all night as we drove around the new district where I lived, so much so that he selected a deserted spot at the end of a dusty street, stopped the car, and switched off the lights. Then he came around to my side, opened the door, and embraced me as he, too, wept bitterly. He took my lips harshly, greedily. I didn't feel his hand until it stole toward my breasts, taking advantage of my stretch blouse. He started to tease my nipple with his well-trained fingers and I went into a wonderful, delicious daze. I came round with a start when he tried to sneak them into my underclothes and I pushed him away like an ill-tempered lioness. He drew back, a cowardly and bewildered cat. He rearranged his ghutra and picked his i'gal off the ground and began to blow the dust off it. As he walked back around to the driver's seat he opened the trunk and took out a heavy briefcase. He handed it to me and asked me to look after it. It was extremely important, he said, and contained all the secrets of his personal and private life. "I have never found anyone I could trust except you," he said. "If I don't come back, you alone deserve to open this briefcase."

I cried for nights on end until there were no more tears left to cry. I was like a desert once watered by sweet rivers that had now dried up; clouds no longer passed over and the parched land howled but no drop of rain fell to soothe it. After four days I remembered his heavy briefcase. I took it out and began to feel it. I could hear his voice inside. I saw him with the Kalashnikov he bragged about. I saw him peering over the parapet of the trenches on the outskirts of Kuwait. I saw him waving his hand that proudly bore the engagement ring I had placed on his finger in the presence of my father and my younger brother, Saad. I saw him waving his platoon on into battle behind him, the silver ring glinting in the air. I saw him a wily commander, a brave warrior, a noble lover. I saw him sleeping fitfully, like a bird, as he dreamed of me.

Should I open the heavy briefcase? Fate tells me no. The tragedy isn't over yet. I remembered instantly the fable of the genie, Sulayman bin Afiya, that my mother used to tell us on cold, dark nights when we were children. I will not go crazy like the sister of the traveling merchant, who married Sulayman bin Afiya the genie. He loved her dearly and let her wander around the palace with forty rooms, and put everything within it at her disposal and command, except for the fortieth room. He told her never to open this room. Never, ever dare to attempt to open it. The briefcase in my hands was like the fortieth room in the genie's palace.

One evening, unable to contain her curiosity, she went to the fortieth room, inserted the strange key into the lock, and turned it. As the door slowly opened and she peered inside, she saw corpses dangling from the ceiling in iron chains, their heads hanging to the ground like butchered animals. She screamed in horror, then put her finger in the hot red blood on the floor and tasted it. She tried to remove the trace of the blood from her finger but she couldn't. She tried to remove the skin but in the end she had to cover it with a piece of cloth. When the genie returned she told him that she had cut her finger while she was peeling the courgettes and potatoes. He realized that she had dared to open the door and seen what he had forbidden her to see. He cast a spell on her, turning one of her legs into the leg of a donkey. Then he took her to an encampment of Bedouin tents and left her there to accept her fate.

No, I will not be the sister of the traveling merchant! I will remain Saleh's sister. Curiosity will not drive me to open the heavy briefcase. I will kill curiosity and bury it out in the open desert where no one can find it. My beautiful soft leg will not turn into the leg of a donkey or a mule or a cow. Perhaps my darling major isn't like the genie, and does not possess the magical powers that will allow him to turn my leg into the leg of a donkey, though he might, in a moment of agitation brought on by the dirty game of war, go berserk and paralyze my foot with a burst of bullets from his machine gun.

I don't know what made me remember the nephew of the corpse washer who washed my grandmother's body, and how he placed his mother in the desert on the recommendation of a learned sheikh, who ordered him not to look behind him when he left her body covered in its shroud on the sand. The sheikh's words aroused his curiosity, just as I was filled with curiosity over the briefcase. He couldn't resist. He was so desperate to know, and when he turned his head to look behind him a bolt of lightning struck his face. The scar remained with him for the rest of his life so he would learn to leave things alone and not to fall victim to the curse of inquisitiveness. I don't know which thunderbolt would smite me if I opened the heavy briefcase, and it really was heavy, as if it were filled with stones. What a clever, wily little private you are! Why didn't your intelligence help you become a major or a lieutenant or even a colonel? I mean, how come they didn't entrust you and your amazing ideas with formulating the plan of attack to liberate Kuwait? They don't need senior ranks to do the planning when you have such a cunning and brilliant military mind, and you're just a private. But then I am your Kuwait, aren't I, and my body is your battlefield?

After more than a week he came back, proud and haughty like one returning from a ferocious battle. On his face was the mark of a violent blow that he boasted he had received in the battle of liberation. I believed it. Indeed, I believed I would be the wife of a brave warrior and an outstanding fighter, in whose arms I would find protection, warmth, and love. In reality he had never left the city, never even left the cells where he was serving a sentence issued by a court martial for his repeated absences, which were spent with me driving around the back streets and conversing in the manner of a major in the armed forces, and flirting with me as infatuated lovers do, while he ignored his working hours and military duties, not as a battle commander, but as a private in the mail corps.

I was desperate to open the heavy briefcase. To this day I don't know what was inside it. Had he put stones in it to tempt me to prise it open and peek at the contents, or forged papers about him and his family, or about the war he had declared on me? I suppressed the desire to satisfy my curiosity so I wouldn't end up like the wife of Sulayman bin Afiya or the corpse washer's nephew. I was too emotional, and far more trusting than I should have been.

23

When I was four years old I suffered from anxiety and insomnia. My mother exhausted herself as she struggled to woo me to sleep. She tried everything: songs, lullabies, and stories, but there was only one song that would have any effect: "Sleep, sleep don't fly away, come hold Manayer every day!" She used to call me Manayer when she sang that song. When she told her stories my eyelids would be wide open right until the very last word. I was filled with pity for the girl who married the genie, Sulayman bin Afiya, and went to live in his palace and opened the fortieth room because she was inquisitive, and saw the corpses hung upside down, and the genie was furious and turned her leg into the leg of a donkey. As soon as my mother reached the bit where the girl was sent away and she hobbled off on her donkey leg, I would burst into tears. The lesson was too much for a four-year-old. My mother used to worry that I was oversensitive—fragile as a colorful butterfly, she used to say. When I grew up this same quality led me to sympathize with a murderer and become her friend.

My manager at the Young Women's Remand Center had already given me a verbal warning about my emotional involvement with the inmates. Then she wrote me this internal memorandum:

To: Social Worker Munira al-Sahi

Due to an exaggerated and inappropriate emotional sympathy that has been noticed in your relationships with some of the residents, and in particular those involved in murder and other criminal cases, I would like to draw your attention to the fact that you should not repeat this behavior, and should establish and maintain a reasonable distance between yourself and the cases you are studying.

I hope that you will take this into account, respect the conditions of your employment, and keep your feelings under control.

Director of the Center

As I read and reread the memo I remembered the case of the Bedouin woman, Maytha. I had arrived at work one morning, almost a year before 13 July 1990, to find an unfamiliar black car at the gate of the Center. Four policemen emerged, followed by a woman chained at the wrists and ankles. Behind her a female guard, arrogant and harsh, goaded her out of the vehicle. I had gone in early that morning, and as the only member of the admin staff there, I had to check the case in and sign the papers from the Central Police indicating that we had taken delivery of her. Then I put her in one of the solitary cells so that she wouldn't mix with the other inmates until she'd been questioned and could be transferred to one of the group wings on the direct orders of the official in charge of her case.

Maytha was a tall, thin woman, her eyes sharp like a hawk's, and in her nose was a zimam with a pale azure stone. She said it was a precious stone that brought her luck, but in reality it had made her luck more dire than mine. She didn't lower her eyes as people shackled in chains tend to do; instead, they darted around the room, taking us in one by one: me, the director, the director's secretary, the psychologist. The director plied her with questions and her personal life unfolded before us as the secretary wrote down her name, age, and place of residence. Maytha voiced this mundane information with boredom and a distaste that reached its peak when she was asked why she had been arrested.

"Surely you must have it written down on the paper," she replied.

"Why did you kill your husband?" asked the director, who had apparently read all the information on the case before she entered the interrogation room.

"Because I hated him."

"Don't you feel any remorse?"

"No, not at all. If he came back to life I'd kill him again."

Maytha's voice was strong and fearless, her confession free and uncompromising. She denied nothing. She had even gone to the scene of the crime at her late husband's farm and acted out all the details of the murder, which she had carried out with the assistance of an Egyptian laborer named Jumaa. A social worker from the Center who had been with her told us how naturally Maytha had committed the murder, gratifying her revenge, deliciously victorious.

Maytha was a young woman in the prime of life, full of energy and affection. She had been in love with her cousin on her mother's side, who was the same age as her; but her father had hated her mother and her relatives, among them this son of her mother's sister, with whom he suspected Maytha was involved in some kind of relationship. The father hastily married her off to an older man who was the same age as himself, although he was wealthy and had a huge farm behind Jabal al-Ramath, near the village of al-Adhaliq. But Maytha didn't love him and her life degenerated into an endless cycle of degradation and abuse. Whenever she ran away back to her family, her father would receive her with a savage beating, and punish her by forcing her to return on foot to her husband. Maytha said that many times on her way back to this hell she had contemplated throwing herself into the well of Ibn Mueed and being rid of the world. "But I always thought about my children, and dreamed that he would divorce me and that I would marry my cousin, whom I loved.

"One time I went back in a really desperate state, my nerves completely shattered, emotionally drained. I found my husband waiting for me with his whip. 'Nothing but a good flogging will teach you, you bitch,' he growled. He whipped me for more than half an hour until I passed out. Then he went and poured ice cold water on my wounds and I started screaming hysterically and the world began to shake. But no one came to help me, neither human nor genie, not even the angels. After all that torture he ordered me to make him dinner. He wanted meat stew and two flatbreads. I could hardly breathe and my chest hurt when I inhaled. Anyway, I made him his dinner. He scoffed it like a wolf all by himself then he stood up and dragged me by my braids to the bed. He jumped on me like a bull and snorted and groaned as he writhed about on top of me. As for me, God alone knows how I felt. And because I was so exhausted and disgusted by the smell of his sweat that was dripping in my face, I threw up. He got up after he'd come and slapped me across the face and kicked me. After that he went to sleep."

Once the bull, as Maytha called him, was fast asleep she slipped out of bed. Her falcon eyes peered into the pitch black night and her pale azure stone glinted in the darkness. She snuck out of the house in pain and overwhelming desperation, and went to rouse the laborer, Jumaa. He had been unable to sleep because of her agonizing screams that had woken the pigeons in their coops and disturbed the palm fronds that swayed in the night. Jumaa knew her tragedy well, for he too suffered the brutality of his master, the old sheikh, and the late payment of his wages, but his desperate poverty left him with no choice but to put up with his lot.

Jumaa prepared the meat cleaver, whetting the blade with the bottom of a porcelain coffee cup. Then Maytha went back inside, leading the laborer, who walked behind her slowly, silently. As he raised the meat cleaver high into the air, the whole of Nature let out a huge cry—the huge sidr tree and the three palms that swayed in the yard, the grass and the mud and the pigeons—clamoring in lament for Cain, lighter of the fuse, instigator of the primordial case of murder. The meat cleaver rose slowly, unsteadily, then fell, swooping down like a rock in the laborer's firm and callused hand. The victim's blood spattered the sheets and the white cotton pillowcase on which his head lay, and the flame of life in the old man's body was extinguished forever.

The young woman, Maytha, and the Egyptian laborer, Jumaa, worked together. They wrapped the body in a woolen blanket and threw it into a very deep pit where even the trained police dogs couldn't find it. The laborer left the country and she returned to the vicious cruelty of her father, who swore that she would never marry her cousin. After the unsolved case of the missing husband was closed, the dead man's brother took her young children to live with him.

Although the children's uncle was plagued by doubts about the disappearance of his brother, he possessed no clear evidence. Then one evening three years after the man had disappeared, he was watching a murder film on the television with his niece when suddenly the girl said, "Like Mama!"

The man couldn't believe his ears. "What?"

"Mama did that to Father," said the seven-year-old. "She hit him on the head and there was a man with her." The little girl's memory was a veritable storehouse of information about the events of that hellish experience as she relived it, thanks to the film. As soon as he had heard everything, the uncle picked her up and took her to the police. There her interrogation began all over again and the criminal investigators put together the threads of the case. The girl claimed that she had seen her mother and a man she couldn't remember beat her father to death, then drag his body in a blanket to the fields. The girl had never uttered a word about the incident she had witnessed and only spoke when she saw a similar scene on television.

Maytha had not thought that her secret would be discovered. How could the apple of her eye, the beloved child who shared her blood and soul and had suckled her milk, testify against her? But the little girl's evidence led Maytha to confess. Indeed, she hardly seemed to care what might happen to her. The life she was living in her father's house was almost as desperate as the one she had lived in the house of her elderly husband, and perhaps there was a life for her in another place.

Maytha laughed a lot, took pleasure in her food and drink, and joked with me as if she didn't have a care in the world.

"How can you laugh when you've murdered someone?" I would ask.

"What should I do? Cry? Isn't it enough I've cried for thirty years?"

"Don't you know that you're going to be sentenced for murder?"

"I know, but so what?"

"But don't you feel any remorse?"

"Not at all. Actually I'm really happy that I got back at him. I just wish I could've gotten back at my father too."

After a long silence, during which she held her head in her chained hands, I asked her, "Doesn't your conscience bother you? You're a criminal!"

"How am I the criminal, ya Munira? I'm not a criminal. He's the criminal, that man who tortured me all the years of my marriage. Between his cruelty and my father's I had no choice."

After she had spent several months with us and turned thirty, she was transferred to the women's prison. She asked the director if she could see me to say goodbye.

"May God preserve you," she said. "Come and visit me in the prison before they execute me. You're the sweetest thing I've ever known in my life."

Maytha cried bitterly in front of us and her body heaved and shook as she sobbed. Then she hugged me for what seemed like forever, and the director had to prise her off me and the guard had to drag her out of the Center. Shortly after, the director sent me that internal memo in order to alert me to my inappropriate behavior.

24

No air raid sirens had sounded in the skies of the gloomy, downcast city for two days. In the overwhelming silence of the house Ali's fingers caressed my flowing hair like the teeth of a comb, and his breath encircled my neck as he mumbled passionate, incomprehensible words. My eyes and my heart were strained toward the door of the men's majlis for fear that it might burst open at any moment, though neither of us expected that to happen. My brother Muhammad was out of town supervising an exhibition of Islamic audiocassettes, now that he was the owner of the largest company producing Islamic audiocassettes and books in the country. Young Saad had asked Father's permission to go out into the desert with his friends. Mother and father were fast asleep, and young Mona would be trying on her dresses, underwear, and heavy perfumes before finishing off with a good dance to "At least I have God, my love" by Muhammad Abdu, and diving naked and panting under a hot shower.

As I said goodbye to al-Dahhal at the gate of the villa, the door was open just wide enough to pop my head around while Ali stood outside on the top step and stole a goodnight kiss before taking his leave. As I closed the door of the house, I motioned to him to close the gate.

Around midnight, I stood in front of the dressing table mirror with its ornate dark brown wooden frame, wearing a lilac silk negligee trimmed with lace and slit up the left side. Just as I was spraying some Chanel Mademoiselle on my neck, I heard a faint tap on the bedroom door. At first I thought I was imagining it but then the light tapping of a knuckle continued. I trembled a little but quickly put on my long silk dressing gown and hurried over to the door, turned the key in the lock, and suddenly saw his beaming face. I almost fainted.

"How did you get in?" I demanded.

"Through the front door, of course," he said as he closed the door and confidently locked it behind him.

"How?"

"I didn't leave. I stayed in the yard."

"So how did you know where my room was? You could have knocked on my father's door by mistake, you crazy thing!"

"Ha ha ha, don't worry," he said as he embraced me then pounced on my face with his lips. I tried to avoid the rough bristles on his chin. I was still in shock.

I pulled myself away from him and stood in front of the mirror so that I could rearrange my hair and adjust the silk dressing gown that had slid off my shoulders. But al-Dahhal stood behind me. He was a little taller than me and he embraced me from behind, crossing his arms around my neck, pressing his rough hands against my breasts and gently squeezing the two little buds. I felt my body gush with readiness, an awesome shudder rousing its pores and hidden places. I felt as though I was entering a trance of overwhelming pleasure. He turned me around and one of his hands continued its wickedness as he pulled me slowly toward the bed and smothered my face and lips with skillful kisses. He sat me down on the edge of the bed and his hand attacked—like a tank homing in on its target—the hills of my chest. His fingers touched my hidden skin for the first time, and as his fingertips stole over me, my breasts awoke in search of ecstasy, while his tongue dealt with the dark recesses of my mouth.

The telephone on the bedside cabinet rang, and I pushed him away suddenly to pick up the receiver in its bear's-paw cover. I brought the conversation with the caller to an abrupt end, "No! Wrong number." I had just hung up—his hand still fondling me from behind as I turned around to face him—when the phone rang again. It was the same voice.

"Who was it?"

"He must have gotten the wrong number then decided he would try and chat me up."

"Why are you so eager to pick up then?"

"The phone could wake my parents up while you're still here."

"Yes, you're right. But where's Mona?"

"Asleep. Why are you asking all this? Don't you trust me?"

"Of course I trust you, but . . . ."

The phone rang a third time. Ali asked if he could answer it and give the caller an earful but I picked up the receiver and heard the same voice whispering, sighing. I was just about to say something when Ali grabbed the receiver out of my hand and started to interrogate the guy. He was on the phone with him for almost ten minutes, and demanded to know whether the man knew the house he was calling, or if it was just a coincidence.

"Why did you do that?!"

"He pissed me off. I couldn't help myself."

"And didn't it occur to you that he might be one of my relatives?"

"Yes, that's true . . . ."

"A man just spoke right after me! What's he going to think?"

"You're right. I'm sorry."

"There's only one explanation. You're in my room. You're sleeping with me."

"But now I'm your husband, according to the law."

"I know. But that's not enough for people. We haven't had the wedding yet."

He interrupted by trying to kiss me, and spent a while attempting to make up but my mood had soured. I had awoken from the delicious daze and couldn't get back in the mood. Moments earlier I had been unable to control myself as I plunged into the well of pleasure. I couldn't help myself.

It was the exact same sentence that Fatima from al-Hasa had repeated when she was being questioned, "I couldn't help myself." She was describing how she had become involved with a university student from a village in the north. Her weeping, as she pleaded with the student at the interrogation to admit that he was the one who had got her into trouble, still drowns out the scent of love in my heart.

25

The souk is quiet at night, like the woman selling children's toys on the sidewalk who appears to have dozed off under her black abaya but she's listening, taking it all in, amusing herself with the sport of a vigilant young man. His eyes are like a hawk's searching for prey as it hovers in the welkin. He spots her and moves in: a ripe young woman, her body almost articulate beneath a black abaya. Their eyes engage in dialogue and conspire together against the little world around them. He looks down at his clenched fist which contains his home phone number. She shakes her head warily, then gives him a chance as she slips away from her mother and her two little brothers over to a quiet corner of the clothes shop, Elegant Woman, and pretends to feel a soft silken blouse between her fair hands. He wanders over and as he passes she stretches out her fingers to snatch the seven scribbled digits.

Their voices circle in the city sky and keep the darkness awake all night as they become acquainted with one another's mischievous souls, hellbent on passion and love. Her name is Fatima. He has two names, as usual: one for his ID card, his university, his family, his relatives and friends, and a professional name for hunting hungry, adolescent women—Bandar. Now that's a perfect name for a wealthy young man from an old aristocratic family. Mueed, on the other hand, isn't as suitable for making the acquaintance of young women as it is for seeking state benefits or a grant to buy a piece of land.

Everything in this city carries contradictions, as if it is made up of entities broken into fragments. Inside each individual there are two persons, the ectoperson and the endoperson. The one on the surface is respectable, polite, sincere, and open, while deep inside numerous other personalities lurk: thieves, traitors, bigots, and puritans. People change these inner personas just like they change their clothes, according to the weather, the place, the situation.

Mueed didn't reveal his name because he was ashamed. He was keeping his true identity a secret, just as he did when he wrapped his shmagh around his face and put on his cheap sunglasses in order to go unrecognized. Fatima, on the other hand, who also went unrecognized in a black abaya with embroidered edges, was taken in by promises of marriage and a home, and dreams taller and more distant than the crown of a Hasawi palm tree swaying in the wind. And so it was that she found herself, apprehensive and confused, sitting next to him in his little old Honda, his hand clasping her cold one and suffusing it with a warmth it had never before known.

"Where are we going?"

"The souk."

"Why?"

"To choose the wedding ring."

She did not suspect that her boyfriend, Bandar, whose voice she had been addicted to for months, was simply casting a line into the swollen stream of her passion in order to entice her, dangling the ring before her as bait so that she, tender and enamored, would bite, only to find her mouth swallowing the sharp point of his hook. He told her that he had left behind in his apartment a very important gift that she had to receive. As soon as they were inside the humble residence he pounced on her like an expert fisher of women, taking her trembling lips, two juicy fish flapping in his basket.

He embraced her for a long time, and convinced her that he needed some time to gain his family's approval and see to his affairs. Fatima was young and he knew how to seduce her. He lay her down quickly on the living room sofa and sank his hook into the deep water, disturbing its quiet stillness, and releasing into it the seed of a lost and terrified minnow.

"I couldn't help myself."

Fatima howled and wept during the interrogation as Munira al-Sahi the social worker—who sat on the fourth chair beside the investigator, the ministry representative, and the clerk—tried to console her.

Early one morning, in her third month, Fatima suddenly felt an agonizing pain. Her small family took her to a private hospital. The parents were astonished to learn that their young daughter, who had blossomed like a rose, was carrying in her womb an unexplained thorn. The Syrian doctor's private clinic wasted no time in informing the hospital police about the case of the young woman who had conceived without her family's knowledge, while Fatima wept hysterically. She had spent more than two months looking for him, but the number that bore the soul of her beloved had turned into hell and only the king of torment replied, denying there was anyone there by the name of Bandar. The apartment was empty, no longer any Bandar or Mueed or any other bastard there. Even his colleague who owned the apartment denied that he had ever known him, and suggested that young Fatima's memory was impaired and that she could not be certain of the location of the place in which she had been deflowered.

"Please, Lord, let my family forgive me!"

The interrogation was interrupted many times, whenever Fatima burst into tears, imploring the ever watchful but distant Almighty. The investigators would fall silent for a moment before resuming their questions while Munira al-Sahi's fingers kept slipping under her niqab to wipe away a warm tear that slid helplessly from her eye. It never occurred to her, not even for a moment, that years later in her maturity, she too would become involved with a man who had two names, Ali al-Dahhal and Hassan bin Asi, who had more than one job—a major in the army and a private in the mail corps; more than one personality, more than one face, more than one family.

Did not the Arabs long ago take pause before a journey or prior to an important undertaking to carefully consider the omens? Didn't the desert dwellers take account of all the signs that guided them in their lives and along the manifold paths they followed? How on earth had Munira al-Sahi not noticed a sign like that as she took part in the interrogation of an abused adolescent girl? How had she, a grown woman, let herself fall into the snare of Ibn al-Dahhal, who, let it be admitted, was a far more intelligent and experienced tactician than the scam artist who had seduced Fatima?

The living room sofa was green, with thick well-worn cushions. He had intercourse with her two times then retired naked to the bathroom, taking his vest and long white summer underpants with him, leaving his thobe in a heap on the living room floor. At this point Fatima's female inquisitiveness got the better of her and she grabbed the thobe. In the pocket she found his wallet. She was stunned to see on his university ID his real name under his smiling photograph. She couldn't make up her mind if he was smiling for the photographer or if he was laughing at her.

"Good Lord, what has he done to me?"

Her inconsolable tears poured over the tiles of the interrogation room, as she sat there encased in her abaya like a little insect caught in the vast web of a spider, his many legs slowly moving toward her. Her body began to shake with fatigue as the investigator, the ministry representative, and the clerk silently entered the room.

"What is the name of the person you became pregnant by?"

"I knew him as Bandar."

"Do you know his real name?"

"His name's Mueed . . . ."

She broke down once again as she related how she went through his clothes while he enjoyed the cool water of the shower gushing over his victorious body.

Munira attended the next session, having taken her morning shower to wash away the sleep but without using her favorite jasmine-scented shampoo, or putting on perfume, or lining her wide eyes with kohl and filling in the lids with shadow. She did not want to attract the attention of the men: the investigator, the representative, and the clerk.

The room was quiet, having hardly had the time to rub the morning sleep off its tiles. The voices of the investigator in his spectacles and the clerk were drowsy and subdued. Then, just as the ministry representative handed Munira a folder with copies of the previous session so she could file them away at the Remand Center, there was some commotion outside the room, and a weary face with disheveled hair peered through the door.

"The bitch, damn her!"

The policeman bundled him into the room and the chains around his ankles dragged along the floor. He raised his cuffed hands toward the young girl.

"Who are you and why are you blaming me for the mess you're in?"

"How can you say that? I'm Fatima. You said you loved me." She was about to get up out of the chair but the investigator ordered her to sit down.

"What happened to your promise to marry me? We were in love."

She showed him the ring, the bait with which he had captured her young and trembling heart. "Look. This is our wedding ring."

Bandar or Mueed didn't look at her, just muttered something contemptuous under his breath. The investigator motioned to the representative and the clerk to leave the room so that the two youngsters might have a chance to be alone together with Munira so that she could bring to bear her social and psychological skills on him. Fatima wept in front of him and implored him for decency's sake and the name of his tribe to marry her. Munira reminded him of the wrong he had committed in the destruction of this small family, and how his denial could lead to her imprisonment and his expulsion from the university.

"Protect me just for a month. Marry me, if only for one week."

He shouted arrogantly, and denied he even knew her. "I'm a student, I have my studies to worry about! Go ask the guy you really slept with!"

All she could do was cry and pray and beg and beseech.

Fatima's stunned father had taken one month's unpaid leave from his job as a cashier in a large building contractor's office and had given himself entirely over to his tragedy. His feet almost wore a path in the pavement as he paced up and down outside the prison, pleading with the young man to atone for his crime, sometimes beseeching him, at other times tempting him by offering to bear the costs of the wedding. He said he was even willing to accept a secret wedding, without the boy's family in Ha'il knowing anything about it—all to no avail.

The investigator was experiencing a growing sense of irritation with nothing to go on and no clear leads in the case.

Munira al-Sahi was no less despondent, for she could see herself in the desperate young Fatima.

"Do you have any evidence to prove that this is the young man who made you pregnant?"

It was not easy for the bewildered young woman, beguiled by the love that had left her mind spinning, to remember anything that might help her. All she could do, when the investigator asked her why she hadn't defended herself, was repeat the phrase "I couldn't help myself." She looked around the room, then toward the window as if she were expecting some kind of inspiration. Suddenly she cried out, "Yes, I remember!"

All faces turned toward her, even his, though he had spent all day avoiding her eyes, and the chains on his feet and hands rattled.

"There's a dark mark on his left shoulder."

"What is it exactly?" asked the investigator.

"It's like a tattoo, or an old burn."

"What do you have to say?" asked the investigator as he looked at the youth.

"She's lying!"

"You're the one who's lying, you criminal!" shouted young Fatima.

"Take your clothes off," said the investigator quietly.

There was an awful silence after the investigator had addressed the young man, who was very reluctant to proceed with the ministry representative, Munira, and the clerk present. Munira stood up to leave the room but the investigator ordered her to sit back down, explaining that the members of the investigating committee should be privy to everything, in order to sign the report on the basis of a thorough acquaintance with the facts.

The boy struggled out of his thobe, and stood in his vest and long white summer underpants. Then he removed the white vest and the scar of an old burn shone on his left shoulder. Suddenly he felt a violent kick in his backside. The investigator had leaped out of his seat in a rage and set upon him, punching him until he fell to the floor.

"Bastard!" he screamed. "Despicable animal!"

Once the ministry representative and the clerk had calmed the investigator down and sat him back in his seat, the investigation resumed and the young man confessed to his crime. Attempts were made to persuade him to resolve the issue and to avoid the tragic business of punishments.

"You mean I'll have to marry a Hasawiya?"

He was reluctant, and his family even more arrogant, insisting that it would be difficult for him to marry this girl. He was sentenced to four months in prison and she was ordered to spend a year in detention away from al-Hasa, which was reduced to nine months because of her good behavior in the institution and thanks to the reports written by the social workers, one of whom was Munira al-Sahi. She had asked her colleagues to look out for Fatima and she kept abreast of the case over the phone in an effort to help heal the poor girl's deep scar. Little did she realize that she herself would suffer a wound that would take an entire lifetime to heal.

26

After she finished studying sociology at university, Munira al-Sahi spent two stifling years in the house. Then she spent barely a single term as the student counselor at a government school before she decided to hand in her resignation. The headmistress, Madam Tharwat, had plied her with requests and insults, even ordering her to arrange desks and chairs in the classrooms with the Filipino janitors. In the end she had spat on the headmistress's desk and slammed the door behind her. She got over it eventually, even though she continued to consign painful stories to the bottle. Perhaps one of the strangest occurred on the first day of her job as a social worker at the Young Women's Remand Center, which she began after spending four years in respectable unemployment.

It was a day I will never forget. The director and my colleagues insisted on my joining them for breakfast; they used to call the thrashing of the young girls "kidney for breakfast." As we walked down the corridor I told my colleague that I didn't like kidney or liver. She poked me in the ribs and her fat body shook with laughter. "This is fresh kidney. You'll love it. No one misses it!"

At that time I had just started as a journalist, writing a weekly article for the newspaper under the title "Love and Ink." It had made the director of the Remand Center a little reluctant to accept my credentials.

"You're a journalist. How can I be sure your curiosity won't get the better of you?"

"What do you mean?"

"We have cases here that can't be written about. They should be treated with the utmost confidentiality."

"The press doesn't publish these things anyway."

"I know. I'm just putting you in the picture."

"Insha'allah."

The corridor was long and resembled the belly of a dead snake. The walls were lined with narrow windows that had iron bars on them. As we stopped at an iron door clamped shut with a bolt and fitted with locks, I snatched a quick look at the two strapping guards. I felt puny and insignificant in their presence and as I looked at their biceps I was reminded of the terrible guardians of the magic lantern. They opened the door for us and we went through, the fall of our footsteps on the cheap broken tiles shattering the silence. We stopped again at another door, and another, until eventually we emerged into a wide room with high walls. On all sides, tiny women covered in black were huddled together, all leaning against one another in search of protection, without sound or movement or breath. The silence was absolute, asphyxiating, and as we approached them they seemed like beasts at the slaughter. A couple of minutes later, one of the guards at the door called out.

"The Sheikh's here."

"Which sheikh?" I asked my colleague next to me.

"The one who will oversee the implementation of the sentence."

"What about breakfast?"

"What breakfast?"

The sheikh entered, with venerable beard and fine brown cloak. He was followed by a representative from the police and another from the Commission for the Promotion of Virtue and Prevention of Vice. I prodded my colleague.

"Why are they doing this in front of everybody?"

"That's what the law says."

"Why?"

"So that their punishment will be a warning to the other inmates, stupid!"

She said it with the exasperation of someone who had lost all pleasure in the kidney and liver breakfast. I decided to keep quiet and see what happened. Then the sheikh's voice broke the silence as he asked for the names of those who had been sentenced to flogging.

Another voice began to read them out, "Haila Muhammad, partaking of intoxicating liquor and running away from her family." A diminutive body in an abaya stumbled forward into the center of the room. As it rose toward the lofty ceiling, the whip whispered sadly and averted its perturbed eyes before descending with a hiss that cut the angry air. A stifled sound issued from behind the black garment as the girl attempted to extricate herself from the hands of the inmate who was holding her in place. The voice of a third man threatened that if she did not control her pain and her voice, he would lose count and have to start the flogging all over again.

I had studied sociology and the origins of punishment in the lecture halls at university. I had learned about the moods of the human mind and the subconscious, and the psychology of the wrongdoer, and so many other things from experts and scientists whose names and theories had flown around those huge chambers. How on earth, Lord, could I spend so much of my life absorbing that stuff just to see it all blown away in seconds? I felt like a frivolous little girl throwing paper planes, made black with all the writing, the thoughts and ideas of middle-aged men who had spent their lives in laboratories, poring over their experiments. Now their work was being torn to shreds by the groaning swish of the whip.

"How can you let this happen? It's degrading, it's torture!" I blurted out in spite of myself. I couldn't believe what was happening. But then I felt my colleague squeeze my wrist.

"Don't you worry about a single one of them."

"Why not?"

"You'll soon see."

"What do you mean?"

She didn't answer, and after the three men had wrung their hands and hurried out and the huge door had been closed behind them, the room filled with howls of hysterical laughter. The girls threw their black abayas to the floor and erupted into a stream of lively banter punctuated with giggles as they mockingly hugged the ones whose bodies had trembled like birds under the whip.

I looked on in astonishment like a fool, mouth agape in disbelief, as the girls sauntered in little groups toward the dining room that was situated next door, to eat and continue their conversations with unbridled pleasure.

"Here you have wonders right in front of you!" my colleague continued.

"What do you mean?"

"I mean that these sorts have become immune to flogging and prison and punishment."

Back in the office, the director scrutinized me carefully as she tested my mettle.

"So, Munira. How was the kidney breakfast?"

"Nothing special."

"Nothing special, you say," teased my colleague as she imitated my voice. "Maybe you'd like a bit more chili?"

The director laughed in a rare display of levity then looked me in the eye and advised me to learn to put up with such situations. With time they would become routine. After that I received some perfunctory training on how to open files and check in new cases that had been transferred from the police and the Commission. Two months later I began to supervise the social work in the Center. The theoretical knowledge had gone up in smoke at breakfast on the first day—a breakfast that was to be repeated many times over the following weeks.

I used to leave work at midday and head home. From my back seat in the Ford I would watch the streets and buildings, the minarets and shops, and look at the women walking up and down the sidewalks. I would recall the almost daily floggings in the Center and compare the women who were passing by, their menfolk walking confidently in front of them, with the desperate girls I worked with. Their days were full of sadness and disappointment, and at night they lay awake in the darkness, longing for the safety and security of a real home, not one secure on the outside and on the inside brimming with grief, torment, and desolation.

27

The houses in the city were surrounded by calm. Birds of piety circled above their roofs, and atop their flagpoles banners of certainty billowed in the breeze. Meanwhile, deep inside, fear and anxiety burrowed away, the dank air of suffering hung about their concrete walls, and doubt slumbered eternally in their dark corridors. Old boxes crammed with deceit and treachery cowered in their cellars and cupboards, while lanterns of purity and innocence hung upon their doors.

Munira al-Sahi had only seen the lights of purity in front of the houses, and the birds of piety flying in great flocks over the roof tops, but that first day in her job she stretched her hand into a very deep hole and discovered an alien and unsettling world. It was nonetheless a real world, uncompromising and ever-present. It was just that she was seeing it for the first time.

Her hands delved into the labyrinth of reality, with its bewildering store of secrets, as the meticulous counselor penetrated the depths of the mind in search of the seed of destruction; here was one of the more unusual cases at the Young Women's Remand Center.

The woman lay coiled in solitary confinement like a hibernating snake, sleeping most of the time as she waited for her interrogation to end. She'd been arrested with her husband as they enjoyed an evening of music and drinking with other men and women. Her husband was an obscure folk musician who played the oud. His hoarse voice crooned songs of old folk singers, most of whom had died or become property dealers and real estate agents.

Her voice was slurred as she sang under the influence of the drugs, sitting cross-legged and playing an imaginary oud, delivering the words in a wounded mournful tone:

Everyone loves you, your beauteous guise
You've stolen my mind with your dark roguish eyes.

Late one night, when the inmates were asleep and I was doing the night shift with my colleague the psychologist, I went with the supervisor to check on the rooms. Her voice came floating down the tiled corridor and, because her nose wouldn't stop running, she sniffed as she sang:

Come and have a cup of tea
Just a quick one here with me
Don't listen to what the gossips say
Come on in and leave them be.

She was not aware of what was going on around her, especially on those occasions when she would lie there for ages, motionless as a corpse. This would worry the supervisors and they would have great difficulty waking her up so that she could pray or go to the bathroom or attend her interrogation sessions. The director suspected that the supervisors on the night shift were up to something and that drugs were reaching her from outside the Center, especially given the excessive bouts of sleep that would overcome her. The director ordered that she should be searched again. They stripped her completely naked and made her walk across the room with her legs open like an upside down V so that any concealed cigarettes or drugs would fall out of their hiding place.

Despite this, Hasna, for that was her name, successfully passed the search. The director ordered that the case be put under close surveillance, as she had now developed serious doubts about one of the supervisors on the night shift. The woman had been noticed getting very familiar with Hasna, and she spoke grudgingly about everything, was bitterly sarcastic, and sometimes made rude comments, but after two consecutive nights the supervisor had given away no indication of dubious or unusual behavior.

In the early morning, the footsteps of the Filipina nurse roused the long, sleeping corridor from its slumber. In her hand she carried a small box so she could draw a sample of blood from Hasna—who was lost in a peaceful and fathomless sleep—and take it to the small laboratory at the corner of the building.

When the Filipina nurse placed the result of Hasna's blood test on her desk, the director could hardly conceal her amazement, and questions perched on her eyebrows like a brood of crows on electricity cables. "Good Lord! How did the drugs get into her blood, damn her!"

Hasna's body was like a cadaver as they dragged her down the corridor, and she was not at all happy at being roused from her dream world.

"Why do you enjoy tormenting me so much?" she slurred.

"Who gives you the drugs?" asked the director.

"Oh God. What's the matter with you? Why are you giving me a hard time? Let me sleep."

Hasna was flying, dreaming, conversing in her unseen world. None of us could understand a thing, let alone reach a conclusion or even identify a thread that might lead to a conclusion. We found the maintenance man and he removed the light bulbs in her single cell one by one, pulled the air conditioning unit out of its frame, and took up the carpet, but there was nothing there. Even among her clothes and personal belongings, and in the adjoining bathroom she used, and in everything that had anything to do with her, we discovered nothing that could explain all the drugs in her body.

A little after midday came another difficult surprise for me, the new employee, and it was no less cruel than the ritual of kidneys for breakfast had been on my first.

"Full body search!" announced the director.

I was one of the members of the search committee. We went into Hasna's cell with the director, the doctor, the psychologist, and four wardens. The wardens lay their victim out on the floor, two on each side holding her legs as wide apart as they would go. The doctor coldly put on her gloves, and another warden who had just arrived proceeded to remove Hasna's underwear as she screamed with a vicious awareness that I heard for the first time,

"Let me go, you animaaaaaals!"

She was unable to resist as she writhed about helplessly, drained by the effect of the drugs, especially against the four strapping and determined wardens. The doctor set about her business inside Hasna's vagina and in less than a second we were amazed to see her pull out her hand, hesitantly, like a mouse emerging cautiously from its hole, tugging a long strip of pills that were all stuck together from the moisture.

Hasna wept inconsolably, banging her head against the walls as the effect of the drugs began to wear off. She refused to eat or to take her medicine, and when she was force-fed she stubbornly and hysterically struggled not to chew.

"How could you keep those pills in such a sensitive place?" fumed the director. "You know it's dangerous. You could die from poisoning!"

"No, no, no! The place is wide enough, full of blessings. God grant strength to those who widened it!"

She didn't stay long in the center. When we learned that she was in her thirties she was transferred to the main Women's Prison. Hasna didn't have a clue what was happening. She had never been fully aware of reality for any length of time. Whenever she felt the drugs wearing off she would pull a white pill out of her secret stash then return the rest to their damp hiding place.

I was mindful of all this as I pondered how people live two lives, one for others and one for themselves, in which they indulge in their private deeds and deviations. A public and permitted life and another secret one, buried in the depths of cellars and souls and dark subterranean vaults, just like those white pills that only skilled fingers—sightless though they might be—can locate.

28

I was lacking sight myself when I bumped dizzily into love, blinkered by emotions and desires that had lain dormant in years past. For despite the remarkable experiences through which I had discovered the hidden chambers of the society around me, I was not able to grasp a single fleeting moment of light during my obsession with him.

Love was blind as a bat as it flew around my dimly lit room one sad night at the end of July 1990. It slammed into the dressing table mirror and landed on its back in the thin trickle of light seeping through the window. It took off again and knocked over the bottles of perfume that stood in a row on top of the dressing table, swerved sharply, collided with the lace fringe of the lampshade, then set off once more, stung by the heat of the bulb that had just been turned off, only to land on the striped linen summer sheet. I picked up the lovesick bat and sheltered it under my sheet. I spent the night whispering in its ear with all the passion of a thirty-year old woman deprived of love and soft, sleepy little words that make the heart race in a wild turmoil of rapture.

"I love you," he had told me for the first time.

It was the end of July and Iraqi tanks and armored personnel carriers were mustering on the outskirts of Basra. At the same time Ibn al-Dahhal's armored feelings were aiming their ammunition toward my soul, firing twenty-one shells into my weak and yearning heart. A few days later, little Kuwait had become the nineteenth province of Iraq, and I the eighth belonging in al-Dahhal's undisclosed possessions, along with six children and a wife.

It never occurred to me, not even for a second, to search the glove compartment of his car, or the pockets of his military jacket thrown in the back seat, or to let my feminine intuition unearth more of Ibn al-Dahhal's secrets, as young Fatima from al-Hasa had done on her first and final meeting with Bandar, whose real name was Mueed. She found evidence of his true identity in a rare lapse of concentration on his part, as he closed his eyes under the burst of cold water from the shower, after he had emptied his hot water into her well.

How many times had al-Dahhal gotten out of the white Cherokee to buy a juice or a Turkish coffee, and my hand had failed to reach for the glove compartment that was almost touching my knees, where I might have discovered a bill or his personal identity card or even the birth certificate of his youngest child. But I had thought it would be a transgression, an unjustified misbehavior, and I had made up my mind never to do it.

The golden opportunity slept in my arms for almost a week: the black Samsonite briefcase, which al-Dahhal had left for me to look after until he came back from Kuwait.

"Guard it carefully!"

"What's inside it?"

"My secrets, personal things." Then he added, "There's no one else I trust like you to leave my secrets with."

"Okay. Where are you going?"

"Kuwait."

"What for?"

"We're going to get an important person out."

"Who?"

He didn't answer, of course, as usual. He considered such matters confidential and he was not allowed to divulge them.

It made me imagine I had an important fiancé who played a key role.

I was a woman with a will of iron. I could keep my impulses in check, shoo away the birds of curiosity that circled above me, and prevent my fingers from feeding them the seeds of inquisitiveness, the desire to uncover my fiancé's secret and duplicitous life.

For not only was fate weaving its trap for me; I felt it was slapping me on the face whenever I came close to discovering the truth so that I would miss something. I failed to notice the plastic bird dangling from the rear-view mirror of my brother's car when Ali came driving it. I didn't realize I was sitting in the car of my brother, Major Saleh, who'd been sent to Britain on a military training course. I even used to call my former colleague, Suad al-Dahhal, quite regularly, and every time I meant to ask her if she was related to Ali, fate seemed to stall my tongue and I never got round to it. I'd ask her what was new at work—she was a teacher at my old school—or about the eccentricities of the Syrian headmistress Tharwat, then I'd end the conversation.

Lots of times I'd pick up the receiver, snuggle in its bear's-paw cover, and spend a few seconds thinking as I looked at my round angelic face in the dressing table mirror; then I'd put the receiver quietly back in its place. Sometimes I'd even tap in the seven digits of Suad's number but as soon as the phone started ringing I'd reach out my hand sluggishly, reluctantly and replace the receiver. Then the voice of Ali al-Dahhal would bowl me over, mellow and thick, adorned with loving words of desire.

29

Three boys, three girls, and a wife!

Like little birds, their mother cuddles them in her safe, cozy nest, waiting for a mate who is always absent. She knows he flies swiftly and with great skill, but she can't be sure that he isn't landing from time to time in a nest other than hers. The beaks of doubt were enough to peck the certainty out of her eyes. True, she'd left school after primary four and been married to Ibn al-Asi; and true, she was killing herself and what remained of the flower of her youth for the sake of those twelve tiny eyes that waited for the absent compassion of their father. She was a tad disorganized and not very clean either. Perfume had never found its way to her bosom, and the only thing that awoke her nipples now were hungry little lips; but she did the chores for him and dutifully washed the corners of the house.

Ghanima, for that was her name, also looked after her children's grandfather, who was forever weeping for the desert he had forsaken, and his animals—a camel and some sheep—that his only son Hassan al-Asi had sold for next to nothing in the city livestock market before taking his father to live with them in the concrete house. It was a small, compact house, not a flimsy mud one or like the spacious new villas, but sufficient for their needs and large enough for the screaming and crying of his six children, though not so big that the Bedouin father's mournful cries went unheard as he yelled "Ya Hassaaaaan!"

In the early morning the children would bounce out the front door and set off on foot for their elementary schools.

The house would fall silent and Ghanima would find some time to go back to sleep, closing the door of her single room on the roof and leaving the old Bedouin downstairs with his bowl of bread dunked in condensed milk. She wouldn't see his face screw up with every slurp as though he were imbibing medicine or poison, or grieving despondently for light-skinned she-camels that had wandered off among the sand dunes.

Ghanima was large and slow like a she-camel, and she was unable to hide the despair that gripped her eyes as she asked Ibn al-Asi about his constant absences.

"You know what it's like in wartime," he explained, pointing out that the nature of his job obliged him to submit to the daily shift system and put in the overtime and that he had no choice but to stay at work, supervising the prisoners of war. In any case, the overtime brought in some extra income, though she was surprised at the cash that had been unusually flowing through his fingers lately, since the war had started.

"That's from the overtime, Thursdays and Fridays!"

It convinced her, and he would sometimes add, "Abu Hamad never sees me short," meaning his boss at work, without telling her that the major had traveled to Britain for six months on a training course. And she never did find the power of attorney form in his pocket authorizing him to receive his boss's monthly salary while he was abroad in order to deposit it in his bank account. She'd started to go through his pockets and wallet after her nose was accosted by the women's perfumes wafting from his uniform. Her whole face was a nose; she had an extraordinary sense of smell. She was always telling herself that God might have taken some of the hearing from her ears but He'd given her a pair of nostrils that could tell you what dishes were being served in the restaurants out on the main road.

Whenever she climbed into the Cherokee next to him on one of their rare family outings, the upholstery would exude an unfamiliar odor, a smell of perfume that disoriented her. It entered her nostrils and seeped into her brain and confounded her calm mind. He did not expect her to ask him about the smell but she could still see the constant nervousness in his eyes that an unwelcome question might land on his head; something like, "There's a strange smell in your car," as she looked straight at him.

"Did my father take his medicine today?" he would ask, evading the question.

Sometimes he would concoct an imaginary conversation in his mind, while she imagined a long argument that would end with him raising his voice, pretending to be angry and disgusted and bored. "Spare us the anguish and go back to your family!" Once her mind got to the shouting part, she'd stop thinking about bringing up the matter of the bewildering perfume.

One evening at the beginning of September, when the sky wasn't lit up by the Patriot missiles, they went out together to get dinner for the children from a Lebanese pastry shop, and to buy some items for the little house that nestled quietly in the Shubra district. As she wriggled about in the front seat in order to arrange her abaya around her legs, she spotted something shining at her feet, glittering like treasure on the mat. She spread her feet apart and bent down to pick up a woman's gold earring. It was the kind that grips the earlobe with a small clasp. She didn't look at it for long before she broke it in her fist, violently, painfully, with a lump in her throat. She didn't know if he'd noticed or not. He pretended not to, though his mouth went dry and he felt an overwhelming sense of guilt and apprehension crawl slowly, agonizingly, across his chest.

How had the damn earring ended up there? Why hadn't he found it earlier in the evening? He'd gotten fed up looking for it, having searched everywhere after Munira had felt her ear to make sure the other earring was still there. It had fallen off during a long, passionate embrace that had culminated in an abundance of gluttonous kisses. As Hassan al-Asi pondered all this, a painful lump formed in his throat and a burning sensation seared his eyes and heart. May all women be cursed, he said to himself. I don't know how they can be so obsessed with details, and see things we men don't see. He stopped the car by the glass door of the Lebanese pastry shop. The door was covered with words painted in bright colors: Homemade pastries, spit-roast Arab shawerma, Abu Zaki pancakes. "What do the kids want?" he asked her.

"Anything." She turned her face away, sniffling. Her nose had begun to run and she wiped away a tear with the palm of her hand.

He slammed the door of the white Cherokee and walked around the front of the car to the glass door of the restaurant. Meanwhile, her fist, swollen with toil, fingers cracked, had just unclenched to reveal a small, shiny gold earring. She stared at it and let out a sad, angry, reluctant sigh. Then she opened her small handbag, unzipped the inside pocket, and stuffed the gold earring inside, as if she were plunging a knife into her own troubled, heaving chest.

Hassan ordered shawerma and some pastries, then pondered for a long time as he watched the Syrian server in front of the column of meat on the shawerma spit. How should he play it now, to put her back on the defensive, where she would be less of a threat? It was as if he were conducting a war, which, although limited in its scope, required experience, knowledge, and considerable tactical ability. How was he supposed to explain the presence of a woman's earring in his car? He felt like a general called to explain the presence of an enemy soldier in his regiment. How could he prove that the soldier was a prisoner who had managed to break his chains and not a spy nabbed with the reward for his treachery still in his pocket? Hassan al-Asi saw the alien earring simply as an enemy soldier who, as a result of negligence, had managed to slip into his camp.

He handed her the bag containing the shawerma, pastries, and a family-size bottle of Pepsi, and she put them down in front of her while he threw the packet of Pampers for his smallest child onto the back seat and started the car. Then he began conducting his maneuver.

"How are you?"

"Fine. It's nothing."

"I was meaning to ask you about your Jameela. Did she get engaged?"

"No!"

He was silent for a moment, waiting for her to ask him why he was inquiring about her sister but she was cleverer than him. She knew where he was headed with this tactical conversation. He started again.

"My colleague Lieutenant Bandar got engaged a few days ago." Then he added, "Imagine, he got engaged to a divorced woman even though he's really young himself. He kept me busy all of yesterday. We must have gone to every gold shop in town so he could choose her shabka and some gifts."

Ghanima understood the explanation he was giving for a gold earring that had fallen unnoticed onto the floor of his car, but she said nothing. Her silence ignited an oppressive anger in his chest as he wondered to himself whether she had bought the explanation or not. Why was she killing him with this silence that shook his trust in himself as an engineer of small battles with women? He wondered how to drive the

141

conversation forward, which sentence might convince her, draw her into an ambush, whereby she would reveal that she had understood his cunning explanation. Her voice, like the gargling of a dying person about to expire, seemed to do away with the need for another decoy.

"Did you take him in your car?"

"Of course. You know, sometimes he's in charge of me. I have to stay on his good side."

He was, for a moment, relieved at the result of this skirmish, and surmised that she was asking in order to figure out whether the earring belonged to the colleague and not to another woman who had sat in the car next to Ibn al-Asi. He had set the ambush well and it had succeeded. But then a thought struck him: had she said, "Did you take *him* in your car?" or "Did you take *her*?"

He decided to say no more as he cursed Munira al-Sahi in his heart. How could she not have noticed the earring, and why had he pounced on her that evening, attending to her lips and ears, which he loved to tease so much, until the earring fell from the lobe into the cracked and callused hand of the wife with the hypersensitive nose? And why, he wondered, hadn't Munira been more concerned about her lost gold earring?

30

Here she is. Here he is. Here they are, the two of them, with so many things to keep them busy.

The final hour gradually approaches. They are building a nest from twigs of deceit, in a tree of little intrigues, and the feathers that line it are forever floating to the ground, one by one. The earth has not closed its huge eye, and watches as the wind blows, trying to scatter the remaining twigs and feathers and their grand dreams.

His white Cherokee pulled up in front of the gate of the Women's Remand Center. He waved a greeting at the cabin window and the guard sitting inside picked up the phone and spoke for a moment. Seconds later Munira al-Sahi emerged, fastening up her abaya and casually throwing her niqab across her face, to which she had just applied a light layer of foundation, and whose lips glowed red, the color of the morning light. As she neared Ali al-Dahhal's car she smiled, not knowing that yesterday he had been called Hassan al-Asi; and not just yesterday, but only a few minutes earlier when he had been standing in his private's uniform, before donning the uniform of Major Ali al-Dahhal.

"A morning of roses to you, my darling," he said as his hand alighted on hers in a soft caress. Her beautiful wide eyes oozed contentment as she gazed at him and he sighed with pleasure. He told her that the Yemeni wholesale perfume shops in al-Batha were much cheaper and had a better selection than the exclusive stores on Thalatheen Street or at the Aqqari market.

"You can get the same brand, the same quality."

"So how's it cheaper?"

"Because they sell wholesale, and the rents on their shops are lower!"

They were silent together as she thought about the kinds of perfume she would chose to adorn the nest she had been promised, while he stared at the tarmac in front of him. A moment earlier he had been looking at Munira's ear—beautifully shaped, sporting a white-gold earring—when the lost earring lying in Ghanima's palm just before he got out of the car to go into the Lebanese pastry shop sprang to his mind. He recalled the silence that had descended upon them as he started the engine, and the bag of shawerma and pastries he had handed to her as he watched for her reaction, and the green pack of Pampers. Suddenly he remembered the diapers. They were still in the back seat. He'd forgotten to take them out yesterday, all because of that damned earring. He wanted to turn around to make sure that they were still sitting behind him on the seat but he checked himself. What if Munira were to turn around now and her gorgeous eyes were to fall upon the pack of plastic diapers that belonged to his youngest child? How would he, a single young man as far she was concerned, explain the diapers? Would she say anything? Would she ask him, or would she kill him silently, with doubt and suspicion dripping from her eyes? Damn these women and the devilish silent questions they concoct, who kill their men with mistrustful looks. A clever, cautious, and masterfully planned exit strategy was needed in order to extricate himself from the snare of the diapers, a plan more brilliant than the one he had contrived for the predicament of the lost gold earring.

"Allaaaaaah," he sighed, pretending to be tired and restless.

"What's the matter?" she asked.

"My sister's having problems with her husband again."

"How come?"

"Yesterday I went and took her and the kids from their home."

"Ufff."

"Every time he drinks too much he kicks her out of the house, then the next day he comes around to apologize."

He felt he had hit upon a wonderful and extremely plausible strategy. This time he had set the trap before the prey arrived; unlike yesterday's earring story, when he had only begun to arrange his snares once the prey already stood before him, free and full of derision for the hunter's stupidity. And as Munira al-Sahi shifted in her seat, turning her back toward the door so that she could console him in his sadness and pain, she spotted the green pack of Pampers smiling cockily at her. Munira stared at them for a moment.

"What's that?" she asked.

Pretending he hadn't noticed he looked into the back of the car, once by turning his head around and then by glancing in the rearview mirror as he checked the large truck following him.

"Look down there! Kids' diapers!"

"Oh! My sister's forgotten Hammoudy's diapers."

He had no idea where the name Hammoudy came from, nor how he made up the elaborate story about the sister and her drunken husband. Skilled indeed was he at directing his miniature battles with naive women, constructing the story of a major in the army, single, whose mother died of tuberculosis when he was a young child and whose father expired some years ago in an accident on the old Hijaz Road. The poor major had a cousin who was in love with him and who cast spells so that he would fail every time he tried to have a relationship with a woman.

Ibn al-Dahhal was a superpower, possessing weapons, intelligence services, and reconnaissance. He would prepare an ambush and scatter grass and leaves over the pit, waiting for a stray gazelle to fall into it. He didn't know if the errant gazelle was Iraq fallen into the trap of Kuwait, or Kuwait fallen into the trap of Iraq. Ibn al-Dahhal understood that the world was all futility and chaos and that he and his deceit were part of it, for he would ask himself sometimes, as he changed from the private's uniform that belonged to Hassan al-Asi into the one that belonged to Major Ali al-Dahhal: who knows who I am? Am I really Hassan or am I Major Ali? What proves it? Papers? What the hell! I can get new papers. Is it the uniform? I can have a major's uniform made that fits me perfectly. So why am I not the real major? Is not the lie that I am a private, and the truth that I am Major al-Dahhal? Who is it that decides our names? Our parents? And do they really own us? Do we have no control over who we are?

"Hello, Major Ali!" cried the Yemeni shop owner, welcoming them in.

He nodded his head in greeting, with the swagger becoming of a major who has his girlfriend or his lover or his fiancée by his side, and she feeling great pride as she rocks on her high heels. Munira spotted a sign in shaky handwriting hung in the window of the perfume shop: "Shop for sale. Owner traveling." She nudged Ali and pointed to the sign.

"Why are you selling the shop?" he asked the owner.

"We have to leave quickly!"

"Why's that?"

"The guys back home are siding with Saddam."

"Is that right?"

"So the government here has decided to expel the Yemenis, because of their government's position."

"I see."

"We've ended up selling for any price."

"May God compensate you."

"May He compensate us all."

And with those words the Yemeni proceeded to show them samples of French perfume on the glass counter in front of him, which was broken and cracked like his own spirit, throwing away decades of toil and exertion like someone who throws dice and doesn't know what it means to get a six or a one.

31

After the dead fall on the battlefield, splattered with blood, their spirits slip away stealthily over the sand. A boy lurks between the trees, excited by the death and the chance of plunder. He removes watches from wrists in which the pulse has only just stilled and plucks from the pocket of one of the dead a wallet, a warm photo of a family that has lost its breadwinner, a few tattered bank notes. One of them bears signatures and messages from children in elementary school who have written, "Baba, don't be long. Baba, we all love you. Don't leave us!"

During the war days, Muhammad al-Sahi differed little from the plunder boy, as he watched the small Yemeni merchants hang signs in their shop windows scrawled in bad handwriting, saying, "Shop for sale. Owner traveling." The Yemenis gave up their businesses quickly, loaded up small trucks with their worldly possessions and their sadness, and headed south in a mass exodus toward Sana'a and the mountain villages of Yemen. All of this made Muhammad al-Sahi—owner of the honey and incense shops and a leading Islamic cassette company—hunt down the fleeing merchants with the same cynicism as the watch boy in the war. It was as if he were playing Monopoly. He bought one shop after another until his safe wasn't big enough for all the contracts and deeds of ownership.

The beating of war drums rises above all other sounds and drowns them out. Nations are like pulsating microbes under the glare of the microscope as they lunge and pitch

blindly between cells. That is how nations make their reso-
lutions, in sympathy with the invasion of Kuwait or against
it, in support of the presence of foreign troops in the region
or against it, with the proposal of an Arab force or against it.
So the Yemenis took to their heels, abandoning the dreams
of a lifetime, moving out of Hillat al-Qusman and the mar-
kets of Ibn al-Dayil where they had abided for so long, while
Muhammad al-Sahi multiplied his profits, snatching the
opportunities that poured into his hands like brightly colored butterflies. He bought the Qasim shoe shop in Hillat
al-Qusman and the al-Khamayil clothes store in Sweiga, then
a perfumery in al-Kabari market. If he had found a humble
stall selling women's accessories in the Mecca souk, he would
have had his hands on it, and his heart and his pocket too.

These were the same Yemenis who decades before would
close their stores, which were scattered through al-Deira near
the clock tower, and whisper to one another about the Siren
of Syria's latest song on television. They would descend
in fanatical droves on the Nile Restaurant, at the corner of
the Ibn Shamsi Building, and sit on all the chairs, listening
ardently, transfixed by the singer's wide kohl-lined eyes that
winked every now and then and made their feeble and impas-
sioned hearts flutter over the tables.

One time, twelve times, your eyes I long to meet.
The iron bridge has broken from the treading of
my feet.

The voice of the diva Samira Tawfeeq floated above the
clock tower while the Yemenis gazed at her and heaved melancholy sighs as she fired lava and shells from her sultry eyes
toward their famished hearts. Silently they sat, their hearts
aching with passion and longing and lust, and every so often

one of them would disappear into the restaurant bathroom for a few minutes, then emerge refreshed, having relieved himself of his amorous urges with a final and decisive groan.

Hamad al-Sahi paid careful attention to the whispers of the Yemenis as they informed one another of the song that was being broadcast on the television. The Yemeni boy, Abdu, used to send coded messages, "You've got the Nashama horsemen today, Mr. Hamad," by which he meant the song that went, "Ya Allah, they poured coffee with lots of spices, poured it for the Nashama on the backs of their horses." Mr. Hamad would understand the allusion instantly, for Samira Tawfeeq, with the round face and wide eyes, had cast the rope of her voice into the well of his heart. Her gorgeous eyes searched out his face among the viewers so that she could shoot him a midday wink and he would sleep peacefully dreaming of her, as he put his arms around her waist atop the mountains of Zabadani. Just at that point, his wife, Umm Saleh, would wake him up and chide him at great length for closing the perfume and incense shop in al-Deira and rushing home just for the sake of a singer. Sometimes he made the excuse that he had a backache and needed to rest. She would advise him to go to his bed but he would insist on remaining in the lounge and ask for bitter coffee. The minute her ungainly body trundled out of the room, he would leap up and switch on the black and white TV to feast his ravenous eyes on the warmth of her wide eyes and her awesome smile. He would feel a rare satisfaction whenever Samira winked at him, as if he were alone with her, sipping coffee in an empty tent in the desert of Najd.

In his small mansion, Hamad al-Sahi would think about the city that was turning into a necropolis surrounded by silence on every side. He remembered the pleasure of the silver screen that had given him a beautiful singer like Samira

Tawfeeq, whom he had loved passionately. She was like a pure-bred Arab mare when her throat trembled, "Ya Allah, they poured coffee with lots of spices." He remembered Umm Kulthum as she sang for hours, her famous handkerchief flapping in her hand, and he would ask himself why they had banned such sweet things after 1981. Life had turned from simplicity to deception. Where were the zoos and the parks where Umm Saleh and I and the children could all go together? Why do we now have to stand outside the park with the Indian and Bangladeshi drivers while only the women and children are allowed inside?

Al-Sahi remembered those Yemenis gathering every Friday at the gate of al-Nasr Club on al-Khazan Street to enjoy the weekly foreign film at the cinema. What cinemas were there now in a city that had become like a mausoleum? Where were the shops that used to sell the songs of Ali al-Ahsa'i and Muhammad Abdu? Where was Strings Music Emporium on New Shmaisi Street, now replaced by the Deeds of the Islamic Martyrs cassette shop? He thought of those music stores and how they had all turned into centers of Islamic propagation. He remembered his middle son's return from the mountains of Afghanistan, lean and gaunt, sporting a long beard. He recalled the conversations they had had, Muhammad's refusal to work for the government, and his shock when his son told him, "I will never work for the Devil."

32

Muhammad al-Sahi was no longer lean and gaunt with a straggly beard. He had grown fat and his beard was neatly trimmed. He wore a clean, carefully ironed shmagh without the customary black i'gal on top of it. His hands were constantly fingering his sandalwood prayer beads and there was always a fresh toothpick protruding from his mouth as he checked his face in the rearview mirror of his lime-green Mercedes.

He told his father that the entry of foreign forces into the country was sacrilegious, tantamount to collaboration with the enemies of Islam. It was not permitted for infidels to enter the lands of the Muslims. They should be expelled as ruthlessly as possible. It was also imperative to remove those secularists and modernists who were in league with the infidels, and to expose the whores and harlots who were demanding their rights and driving cars, inviting fornication and adultery to spread among the women of Islam. He would say all this sitting next to his elderly father as they both leaned on the cushion placed between them. But then he would be caught unawares by his father's snoring, and the old man's head would slump forward onto his chest.

Muhammad al-Sahi would not leave his family alone. He brought home audiocassettes and pamphlets about the torment of the grave, and about collaborating with infidels and Jews. His voice was loud and overbearing, and his two sisters, Munira and Mona, endured it constantly, as did his younger brother, Saad, whenever Muhammad saw him wearing jeans and a T-shirt or listening to music on his headphones.

"You'll turn into a woman, putting oil on your hair and listening to that nonsense." Then he added, "Molten lead will be poured into your ears while you lie in your grave."

Like a vicious wolf in a cage Muhammad al-Sahi paced up and down the living room in front of his silent younger brother, while the poor sad mother was caught between the war of missiles and air raid sirens outside the house and the missiles her son Muhammad was firing at everyone else in the family.

"Maybe tomorrow you'll draw a tattoo on your arm like the infidels do."

Saad said nothing.

"What are those pathetic foreign words doing written on the back window of your car?"

He didn't go home very often, but when he did he went through the house from top to bottom. No one could argue with him. Even father had turned into a silent and passive lamb.

"Can you tell me how this was allowed to happen?" he asked his father as Munira lay catatonic in her bedroom the morning after the wedding to Ibn al-Dahhal had turned into a requiem and unleashed a major scandal.

"If you had been stricter with your daughter and not let her live how she likes, and write that rubbish in the Filth (he meant the press), none of this would have happened."

Muhammad al-Sahi was beside himself with rage as he lurched to and fro, beseeching God to grant him refuge from Satan, and making violent threats about what he would do if his sister were no longer a virgin. If the girl hadn't lost her little treasure, he demanded, then the father should sort the matter out once and for all and give her to the first man who knocked on the door.

When the Sultan became angry that his daughter, the princess, was chasing away her suitors and mocking them—as the popular folk story goes—he decided to give her away without dowry or condition to the first man who knocked on the door. A young shepherd came with a flute and when he began to play, the air was filled with plaintive music. The princess opened her huge window and looked down at the shepherd below. His heart was smitten with her and he knocked on the door, the door of her palace and her heart. And from a pampered princess who lived a life of luxury with servants and rich sofas, she turned into the wife of a poor man who possessed only a flute, whose sad and touching music earned his daily bread.

Munira al-Sahi wasn't expecting a shepherd or a poor man with a flute to turn up. In her case it was more likely to be an older gentleman who already had two or three wives. She would be the fourth and bear him children, who would have more brothers and sisters than even he knew about. She imagined him coming to her every fourth night after she had spent three nights alone recollecting distant days of love and war, dreams and pleasures she would never know again. She thought, after all her brother's ranting and raving, that she might be obliged to make her journalism a refuge—had he not accused her of this?—and become secretly involved with a young journalist who would spend three consecutive nights with her while her aging husband made the rounds of his other wives. During her work with the young women in her charge she had seen cases of women who broke down and wept and others who doggedly resisted and stood firm. She had seen Fatima from al-Hasa in floods of desperate tears, and the unyielding obstinacy of Maytha, who had murdered her old and domineering husband. "If he rose from the grave, I'd kill him again," she had whispered to Munira. Should I do as Maytha did, thought Munira: accept the first man to knock on the door of her father's palace, so that she could prove to her brother Muhammad that she still preserved her little treasure and hadn't lost her virginity?

How many times had her soft hands tried to grasp the threads of the story from the beginning, to spool it all back until she reached the crux of the plot, the inciting incident? Were the accusations of her brother Muhammad against her writing and the weekly column true or not? She remembered that on the night of 13 July she had received a torrid phone call from a reader. Was he just a reader, she had wondered then, or was he a serious admirer of her thoughts and writing? From there the affair had developed into a passionate infatuation with her and her ideas, until Ibn al-Dahhal arrived at the threshold of her young, effusive heart and it offered shelter and shade to him in its widest rooms and most splendid halls. But what had made him go to such lengths to seduce her and lead her astray, to transform himself in front of her into a talented actor performing his role to perfection? Was he feigning love? Munira could find no satisfactory answer. She did not know whom to blame more: herself, or her father, who didn't ask about the man more thoroughly and fully investigate his background. Her father saw the world as all goodness and beauty, and didn't get involved in too many things whether they concerned him or concerned others. He simply preferred to repeat his favorite sentence, "The sheikhs know best."

Should she blame her brother, Major Saleh, who had not discovered the ruse of the private who had stood outside his office door for years? But how was he to know while he was on a course in Britain? He'd even authorized this private to receive his monthly salaries and deposit them in his bank account. But the private had started to live a life of luxury with her brother's money, buying her dresses and perfumes and many other gifts that he showered her with every time they met.

33

He stood in the tea and coffee room between two colleagues, both of them corporals. They were reading an article in the newspaper entitled "Rose in a Vase," by the writer Munira al-Sahi. That morning she had written about the woes of women in society. The two men winked at one another for her brother, Major Saleh al-Sahi, was their superior officer.

Hassan al-Asi sighed as he spoke, "I'm going to marry that girl."

His two colleagues, both corporals, laughed and mocked him about this for a long time. "Wake up, you dumb bastard! You, marry the daughter of al-Sahi!"

He glared at them with unaccustomed antagonism, "I'll marry her, I tell you! You'll see." But the sound of their laughter in the corridor rang in his ears for many days and nights, and they began to have a laugh at his expense every morning, which forced him to think how he could reaffirm his honor after these two fools had trashed it.

Every time he heard the infernal bell ring, he would open the door of the plush office whose windows looked out onto Sitteen Street through heavy, green, drowsily hanging curtains. He would stand in front of the major and click his heels against the deep shag-pile carpet as he saluted, ready to receive his orders for the coming day.

Private Ibn al-Asi spoke cautiously and austerely to his boss, for Major Saleh was not a man of many words. Sometimes even his orders were given through looks, the expression being sufficient for the private to understand what his superior officer required. Moreover, the look would impart whether the major was in a good mood or whether he was angry and irritable. The private's duties were not restricted to carrying plastic files from the major's office to the colonel's, arranging the office furniture, and dusting the major's desk and the coffee table the guests sat at. In fact the moment he shuffled into the room and found the major poring over a file, he would salute with his usual click of the heels and the major would lift one leg on top of the other. Ibn al-Asi would lunge forward toward the military boot, impatiently shaking on the officer's foot, and give it a good wipe with his handkerchief. The major would then exchange one foot for the other so that the private could repeat the procedure.

Hassan al-Asi had never been so insulted or humiliated as he was that morning. He wiped the major's shoes, handed him his glass of tea, and heard a perfunctory mumble, "How are the kids and your father?"

"They're fine, doing well," replied the private pleasantly. "They're always asking about you." He had not intended to say more, but he sensed that the Major was in a reasonably good mood, possibly even ready to indulge in congenial conversation. Al-Asi had thought many times about asking him the question that had kept him up for nights on end.

"Is the writer Munira al-Sahi a relative of yours, sir?" he said in a bold and clear voice. Instantly, the sole of the boot that he had been so assiduously wiping only seconds before thudded into his chest and he tumbled backward across the floor of the office.

"See to your work, private!"

Hassan al-Asi scrambled to his feet and brushed the dust of this crushing and ignominious defeat off his uniform, but before he could turn around the major spat, "You are never again to ask about things that are none of your business!" And as he opened the office door, which seemed heavier than usual and issued a sad creak, he heard the last sentence, like salt on his wound, "You'll do an extra shift for your insolence, Thursday and Friday. Now get out, private!"

I shall carry out your orders, major, but I will do what I have to in order to put an end to your arrogance and have my way with your honor. Private Ibn al-Asi uttered these words to himself as he walked down the corridor toward the tea and coffee room. He paused before entering, and then turned down another corridor to the toilets, where he stood in front of the hand basin and looked at his reflection in the mirror. He contemplated the face for a moment, and tried to locate some of the features he had known when he still had some dignity, but all he saw was a broken man looking back at him with sunken eyes.

"You're a despicable, cringing coward!"

"But this is my bread and butter, my livelihood."

"You're a slave to the job, ya Hassan!"

"But it feeds my six children."

"You're a slave to your children, ya Hassan!"

"No, it's not like that. But I *am* responsible for them."

"When was the last time you saw them?"

"Who do you mean?"

"I mean honor and dignity, or have you forgotten them forever, put them in your file at work and closed it, never to open it again?"

"But I can't do anything or I'll lose my job."

"Yes you can!"

"How?"

"Munira!"

"What about her?"

"Make her fall in love with you."

"Then?"

"Then make her confront her family and take them on for your sake. Get her to challenge the arrogance of that egotistical bastard until he wipes *your* boots."

"And will she accept a private, a mere guard?"

"That's up to you. Use your brain! Where's your ingenuity?"

After Hassan al-Asi had finished his conversation with the man in the mirror, he washed his face thoroughly and began to rouse his cunning imagination: he would, very soon, take charge of Munira, like the commandant of Baghdad. He would invade her heart with armored cars of love, sweep across her body with tanks of desire, and fire a thousand shells in a sudden blitzkrieg of passion and lust, just as the man in Baghdad had done. Hassan al-Asi began to make his way along the highway to Munira's heart on 13 July 1990, just seventeen days before the armored cars and troop carriers set out from Basra to Kuwait. At that point he still hadn't come up with the false name; rather, he was attempting to ascertain the degree of love and desperation in his prey, Munira al-Sahi, for he sensed a certain intoxicating sensuality in her voice that evening as she sat alone at home, having told her mother, sister Mona, and brother Saad that she was too busy with her dissertation to go out with them. Her voice was not normal as it seduced his eager, yearning ear. It was the voice of someone who had been silent for many hours, drawn out and drowsy, seductive and confident, "Hellooo." She was not unsettled upon hearing the voice of a man apologizing for the disturbance. Indeed she responded coolly and flirtatiously, "Who is it?" Thus was Ibn al-Asi able to take hold of the reins and commence battle by extolling her articles, her wonderful ideas, and her tender words. "I really wanted to hear the voice of the woman who wrote those marvelous words," he declared, and added, "but to be quite honest, I did not expect her voice to be so soft."

Every time Hassan al-Asi cast a stone into the pool of her quiescence, the door of her heart opened a little further, and she gave him more space to express himself, until he assailed her the next day with the poems of Nizar Qabbani. Thereafter his nocturnal phone calls began to grow longer. Love's butterflies fluttered about her fabulous ears for hours on end, and she stayed up until dawn. Then the Gulf War broke out. Her Gulf War, however, had already begun.

It was no surprise to him when she asked, "Can you tell me more about yourself?" That was when the fictitious character of Ali al-Dahhal came into being, the mysterious major who was preoccupied with the challenges and secrets of the war: the war against the invaders of Kuwait, as she understood it; the war against her heart that had opened itself up to the upheavals of violent love, as he knew it to be.

34

"We'll miss you, Major Saleh."

Ibn al-Asi embraced him for the first and last time. Major Saleh al-Sahi had prepared his papers and handed the private a signed and stamped letter.

"What's this?"

"Power of attorney."

By 10 July, according to Hassan al-Asi's reckoning, all the spoils had fallen into his hands. Major Saleh was traveling to Britain on his course and had authorized him to receive his salary so that he could deposit it in his bank account. The city was emptied of everything that could stand in his way and he moved about freely, setting snares here and there to trap his beautiful quarry, Munira al-Sahi.

The game began in the tea and coffee room with his two colleagues reading the article about women's issues in the column "Rose in a Vase." It shifted into sarcasm as the colleagues mocked his grandiose dreams of winning the heart of the daughter of an old and respected family. It grew more serious after that unforgettable kick in the chest that had left his heart gravely wounded and his manhood in shreds. For despite the fact that he was a simple man who dreamed of nothing more than a home, children, and a decent life, he had his dignity, and it had been sorely insulted. The implementation of the grand strategy began on 13 July and moved into full swing when Major Ali al-Dahhal dropped into her world, a knight in shining armor come to the rescue of the beautiful princess Munira. Besotted at the sight of his flying white charger, Shooting Star, she leaped up behind him, wrapped her arms around his waist, and threw her enamored head against his back as they soared together above the war-haunted capital to the din of blazing rockets and the bright flashes that lit up the night sky.

As the city slept to the murmur of intrigues before awaking with a long, drawn-out yawn, they'd slip through the streets in the white Cherokee, their resplendent stallion. Very occasionally they'd pass a civilian car, military vehicles that patrolled in threes, and troop carriers towing huge rocket launchers covered in tarpaulin. Foreign soldiers piled into the fast food restaurants. Some were female, blond with braided hair, or black with hair in rows like sandalwood prayer beads. On their backs they carried camouflage khaki rucksacks. Munira did not know what she was supposed to do in the company of a man she was getting to know in circumstances like these. Should she watch what was going on outside, the clamor and commotion of the encroaching war, or should she contemplate the thick hair on his hand as he sat by her side, waiting to strike up a conversation like someone preparing to wage a military campaign?

"Have you bought lamps?"

"Father bought them," then she laughed.

They were laughing about the shortage of gas lamps and how the price had shot up from fifteen riyals to seventy riyals, then to a hundred and fifty riyals for a single lamp. They changed the subject and talked for a long time about the rush to buy adhesive tape, which people were using to seal the edges of their windows to prevent dangerous gases from seeping through in case chemical weapons were fired from Baghdad.

Ibn al-Dahhal was readying his missiles, fitting them with warheads of fraudulent love in order to aim them straight at her fragile, hankering heart. He did not think that this game of his would lead to real love, that he would love her madly and later accuse her in court of using magic, maintaining that he had done what he had done, this whole masquerade, because of a spell that she and an Egyptian woman who worked at the Center had cast. No one knew, not even the judge himself, if he was acting or telling the truth when he fell at her feet in tears and begged, "Forgive me!"

Munira wondered if the setting of the snares began as a scheme to exact revenge, but then turned into true love. All she could be certain of was that he had lied, forged an amazing number of documents, and hired people to help him: one became his brother, another played an aunt who came to the house with him the day of the engagement, and two young women were his sisters. Even shopkeepers and restaurant proprietors addressed him as 'Major Ali.' Did he pay them as well, or did he make do with business cards that bore his assumed name and rank and false telephone numbers, distributing them among the shop owners? Had they also fallen into his trap, just like the al-Sahi family?

Munira didn't talk much as she sat with her sister Mona and their father, having dinner and watching the daily war report. Her father never asked about her fiancé, or whether she met him, for he trusted her implicitly. Ever since he had drowned her in books and made her his wonderful bookworm, he felt she could handle responsibility. His struggle with the senior family members for her to continue writing for the newspaper without using a pen name—she had rejected the idea of changing her identity just to keep them happy—only served to confirm his trust in her. Then she had gone and accepted a man who had made up his name, his job, his family, and his income. How had that happened? And what about those moments of bitter resentment after the plot was uncovered, and his efforts to make up with her the following morning, when she had yelled at him, "Did you also borrow al-Dahhal's dick so you could use it to sleep with me, ya Ibn al-Asi?!"

She had never known such joy as she felt in the week running up to the wedding as they prepared together for the big day. Munira went with him in the white Cherokee and they stood side by side looking at the wedding cakes in the Patchi shop window, seeking inspiration for the one they would create, with many layers of chocolate and sponge covered in whipped cream and various kinds of fruit. They disagreed about the third tier of the cake: she adored the redness of strawberries while he preferred peaches. In the end, the Lebanese assistant suggested a beautiful design incorporating the two fruits. They laughed, and when al-Dahhal teased that the salesman should not add an extra fruit of his own, the Lebanese answered politely, "Certainly not, sir."

She was bursting with happiness as she got out of the car and went into Nesma Women's Photo Studios in order to book the photographers for the big night. They would film the whole thing, from the moment the drums announced her arrival to the cutting of the cake and all the happy moments in between, including her greeting friends and well-wishers. How secure she felt when she was with him. On previous occasions she had refused to go shopping with the Indian driver, not because she didn't trust him, but because of the continual hassle she was subjected to from passersby as she walked alone in the souk and public places, especially as her gorgeous, wide eyes were forever screaming out from behind her niqab.

A few days ago, Munira wrote on a piece of paper that she slipped inside the bottle: "I didn't find my darling Ali in his office and I had to go out with the new Indian driver to choose some tulle and chiffon for the evening dress. He stopped at the Arab Garment Company in the Aqariya market and I went inside. I chose a bolt of pink lace that was really pretty. As I was haggling about the price, the salesman kept looking at my Rolex. After I'd paid him ten thousand five hundred riyals for just three meters of the material, I hurried out of the shop. A young man followed me, trying his luck. He was waving a little scrap of paper at me and saying in a loud voice, 'Take my number, private number!' And when I didn't respond, he shouted, 'Miserable bitch, playing hard to get!'"

35

The fragrant smell of incense hangs in the air.

The place hums with the mumbling voices of the venerable men, their prayer beads dancing between their fingers as they draw their long, diaphanous, brown-and-black mishlahs around them, enfolding the smell of perfume and incense smoke beneath the flowing garments. Boys in gleaming thobes and sparkling white, neatly ironed ghutras stand outside the gate of the large house, carrying incense holders burning scented wood. The men incline their ghutra-framed faces over the white clouds that rise into the air, closing their eyes for a moment as the wonderful aroma of smoldering Cambodian wood fills their noses.

Young men with smiles of welcome on their faces carry brass coffee pots. As they are raised to pour coffee for the guests, the pots twinkle in the reflection of the strings of lights hanging over the small palace of Ibn al-Sahi. The smell of cardamom and cloves and saffron diffuses, and the open courtyard covered in carpets is transformed into a lush garden of smells. Voices fill the courtyard and faces recognize one another as Muhammad al-Sahi, beaming with delight on the occasion of his sister's marriage, announces, "A warm welcome, by God!" while the father's subdued voice—for he has still not fully recovered from his illness—declares to the throng, "By God, what an auspicious hour this is."

It is the twenty-first of February and the evening is a cold one. The women turn up at the al-Sahi household transported in GMCs and SUVs with shaded windows, trailing their perfumes behind them like wistful memories. Black embroidered abayas float about their bodies, concealing crêpe de Chine dresses decorated with chiffon touches, and sparkling strings of precious stones. The women carry small handbags and walk quietly, talking in whispers, but once inside the women's entrance of the mansion, their voices grow suddenly louder and their laughter mingles as they merrily kiss and greet one another.

Just by the door, which is lit up by halogen lamps, Nura and Mona al-Sahi welcome the female guests with smiles that ooze onto the shining Rosa marble floor of the hall. They are surrounded by little girls carrying miniature incense burners, and the hall is transformed into a cloudy white sky by the delicious, fragrant smoke. Every now and then the eldest daughter, Nura, pulls up her black chiffon scarf, which is trimmed with stars and long, soft silken tassels, as it slips off her shoulder to reveal her fair skin. She is wearing a crêpe de Chine dress with a chiffon skirt, tight until mid-thigh, with a triangular slit revealing her leg. Black and white crystal stars are studded along the border separating the crêpe and the chiffon. Nura is mildly embarrassed about her bare left shoulder, which wears only the dress's thin silk strap and is covered here and there by the black scarf with the soft silken tassels. She shifts her hands underneath the scarf and touches the compact leather handbag trimmed in black crêpe hanging over her other shoulder on a long chain with a large crystal buckle. Mona, the youngest daughter, adorer of dancing and singing, stands by Nura's side in an imposing chiffon dress that celebrates her voluptuous figure: widening at the bottom, short in front, and long behind. Colored roses wind up from the hem until they meet at the neck in a large mauve taffeta bloom connected to two leafy branches of green taffeta that twist around her white neck and the diamond necklace adorning it. She walks like a princess, proud and confident, laughing happily, loudly as she exchanges pleasantries with the guests. From time to time she opens her metallic handbag with its mauve inner lining, which looks like a shell adorned with lustrous crystal stones. Mona's frequent opening of her shell-shaped handbag is not intended solely to draw the women's attention to it. She is hoping a man will materialize in its depths, looking up at her with pleading eyes, longing to leap out on his white charger and stand humbly in her presence.

In an upper room, a gaggle of aunts from both the mother's and father's side buzz like a swarm of bees around Munira al-Sahi, while she gives orders. She is seated at the mercy of the Moroccan stylist, who moves skillfully between the hair, which she has braided and pinned up with the scent of roses, and the face, which has been transformed into a Renaissance masterpiece. Her gorgeous eyes, deep, restless seas of seductive beauty, draw gasps of amazement from all who turn their heads in her direction. Munira extends her slender fingers along the arms of the chair so that the Filipina beautician can trim and file her long nails, paint them the color of rubies, and decorate them with diamantine sparkle. When she looks at her moon-like face in the mirror her young heart flutters like a bird about to expire.

She glances at the clock back to front in the mirror. "He's late!" she murmurs apprehensively.

Then the voice of her sister Mona cuts through the commotion. "Hurry up! His aunt and sister have arrived."

The children and young men dart around the male section, serving the guests, carrying pots of bitter coffee and red tea without milk or with cinnamon, or yellow tea with mint. Boys wearing silver- and gold-embroidered tagiyas carry gleaming trays loaded with glasses full of tea and offer them to those guests who are already seated. Suddenly the place erupts at the sound of car horns blaring at the end of the street. Muhammad and Saad al-Sahi rush over to the gate with some of their uncles, calling frantically, "Incense . . . bring more charcoal, Boy. . . . Who's got the scented wood?" Out of a deluxe black Mercedes steps the imposing figure of Major Ali al-Dahhal in a black mishlah trimmed with a thick band of gold and a white ghutra the color of snow. Dispensing smiles among the guests, who greet him with their congratulations, he bends with great humility toward the children to kiss them and ask, in a distinguished voice that issues from the deepest recesses of his throat, in the way the best families speak, "What's your name, my boy?" and turning to another, "Whose son are you, young man?"

Then, like a meteorite hurtles through the depths of space toward an unsuspecting earth, their eyes meet. Private Hassan al-Asi, striding through the crowd masquerading as a major whose name is Ali al-Dahhal, and Munira's cousin Nasir, who works with him at the ministry.

"Hassan!" he cries in amazement as he sees the private coming to marry his cousin with false name, spurious job, and fake demeanor. The groom freezes at the heart of the gathering, halfway between the gate and the groom's throne.

Saad al-Sahi starts while Muhammad stares at his cousin Nasir and his hand roams over his neatly trimmed beard. "What did you say? Nasir, speak!"

They pull him by the hand and take him to one side. Nasir whispers that the man is just a private who works as a messenger and guard at the office of Major Saleh al-Sahi. His name is Private Hassan al-Asi, not Major Ali al-Dahhal. Muhammad decides not to say anything in front of the guests, but his younger brother Saad rushes forward, pulls a small revolver from his cousin's hip pocket, and lunges at al-Asi. He is just about to take aim when Nasir barges into him and snatches the revolver from his hand. "How could you sully your reputation and ruin your life with the blood of this filthy bastard!"

Not all the men, who are scattered around the place, notice what has happened. The two brothers confer with their father's brother and some maternal uncles. "We have to keep a lid on this," says one uncle. Together they decide to keep quiet and let the matter pass peacefully until the guests leave. They order Hassan al-Asi to continue his procession toward the throne, where he shakes hands with some of the invited guests before proceeding in to his bride with Muhammad al-Sahi holding his hand. Muhammad would like nothing better than to drag him into the alley behind the house and plunge into his chest a dagger he keeps with him from the mountain war in Afghanistan. "If I had the Kalashnikov in my hand," he whispers into Ibn al-Asi's ear, "I wouldn't let you get away tonight." Ibn al-Asi's hand turns to ice.

36

When he entered the women's hall, the place erupted in a fit of ululation. My brother Muhammad led him to the throne next to me. They were followed by my brother Saad. When I stood up to receive him, he boldly took my hand in front of my brothers and the female relatives and kissed it warmly. Whistles and shrieks of delight filled the hall, cameras flashed, and he posed with his arm around my waist, then embraced me. I noticed a seething rage buried deep in both my brothers' eyes. I put the anger in Muhammad's arched brows down to the whistling, ululation, and music, which he considered haram, but why was Saad's face flushed red like that? What had made him so angry he was about to explode? Had he been struck by Najdi jealousy over his sister, of the strange man who was about to invade her hands, face, and body? But he was my husband and I loved him. Neither I, nor any of the women in the hall, knew of the scandal that had just erupted in the men's section.

We walked together. I was followed by little girls who carried the long train of my dress. We stopped in front of the wedding cake, the one we had designed together at Patchi. Everyone was standing around us as the three Filipina photographers pointed their lenses in our direction. I picked up the huge knife and he placed his large hand over the whiteness of my two little hands. I wanted to make the first cut in the middle of the cake but he moved the knife toward my name, placed the blade above the letter M, and thrust it in as he whispered provocatively in my ear, "Tonight I'm going to plunge into your pearl!" I blushed with embarrassment. Little did I know that he had killed me with that knife on the happiest night of my life. He dismembered my name. I was no longer Munira on the nights that followed. My flame was extinguished.

My brother Muhammad indicated with a stern look that Ali should leave. As he pulled away he whispered to me that he would be going away on an official mission, and that it might take some time. He kissed me and I noticed no fear, sadness, or apprehension on his face. Just after midnight, my mother and father, two brothers, and two sisters came into my room. Their eyes were like the corpses of birds that had fallen reluctantly out of the sky due to some dreadful pestilence. My sister Mona sobbed silently. My father's eyes swept the carpet dejectedly. My mother sighed as she repeated, "There is no power and no strength except through God."

My heart was thumping, and a sudden coldness attacked my limbs. I did not know where to turn my eyes, which one of them to look at. "What's the matter? What happened?"

My father quietly sat me down on the edge of the chair and said, "Your husband is not Major al-Dahhal."

Out came the details of the scandal that had transpired in the men's section precipitated by my cousin Nasir. Their voices were all raised at once, my mother explaining, my father lamenting, my brother fuming, "God bring him no joy in this world or the next! I hope cancer devours his heart. Father, you ridiculous man, sleeping in your shop! I swear by God, we will kill him."

"She knew what he was up to all along," Muhammad said to them, then glared at me. "You must have known the truth about him, damn you, and you never said a thing. You planned this with him from the start, you whore!"

My brother Muhammad fired his bullets all around the room as he paced up and down like a vicious, baying wolf, aiming first at me then at my father.

"This is the result of spoiling her and letting her do what she wants. This is what blind trust gets you, respected father!"

Then he turned back to me. "Is this the freedom you're demanding in that drivel you write, madam?"

I was struck dumb. My tongue turned to a piece of bone, and my brother like a rabid dog devoured it. I searched in their accusing eyes for a hint of consolation, but all eyes were blaming me.

They stare at me with the look of mourners in their eyes. The white dress hugging my body has become my shroud. Am I dead, I wonder. Are they following my funeral to the cemetery, bearing me in silence on the shoulders of my shame and humiliation while I jolt from side to side on the bier? All I can see is the blue sky above me and birds darting past on light wings. All I can hear is the doleful lament of the mourners as they rush toward the graves. At the edge of the pit intended for me I spy the custodian of the cemetery. There is an Indian laborer standing by his side, piling up the mud bricks that will wall me in the crypt. Ali al-Dahhal is busily digging the grave while my brother Muhammad mixes water from a metal bucket with earth to make more bricks. They take me down from their shoulders and I walk over to the grave and sit on the edge with my legs dangling inside. Then Ali al-Dahhal pushes me forward and I sink into the depths like a cat searching for shade on a scorching day. Al-Dahhal lands behind me and the Indian laborer, who looks like our driver, hands him the bucket of mud so that he can proceed to close me up inside the compartment that is hollowed out to one side of the grave. Then my brother brings the bricks and al-Dahhal skillfully builds the wall. And when the last shaft of light is plugged, the world suddenly turns black.

I had fainted. My brother Saad caught me and they sprinkled water on my face. I woke up and began to weep hysterically. My younger brother Saad hugged me and burst into tears. My sister Mona wailed out loud and Nura sobbed uncontrollably as she held her head in her hands. And Mother, she wept too and mopped the tears with the back of her hand as she repeated, "There is no power and no strength except through God." And then in an effort to console us all, she spoke the verse, "And it may be that ye dislike a thing which is good for you." As for my father and brother Muhammad, we had not noticed them slip out of the room.

A few hours later, just before the first light of dawn appeared on the horizon, I was stretched out on my bed, eyes wide open, mind completely shut down. I could not believe what had happened. It was as if I had learned of the death of a dear friend. I remembered my grandmother for a moment and how I continued to see her sitting in her room for days after she'd passed away. Every time I went in I'd realize she'd managed to sneak in before me and there she would be, sitting smiling at me, as if she hadn't died at all.

Unbelievable. 'Major Ali al-Dahhal' was no longer my beloved husband. My husband was Hassan al-Asi, a private, who had been married for thirteen years and was the father of six children. It was unbearable. I had seen him a few hours earlier, a young man, resplendent groom, high-ranking major, from a good family. Then I was told that he had ceased to be. As if a dear friend, who was with us minutes before, joking and chatting, had had a heart attack and died.

When the phone rang just before dawn the ring was not the neighing of a horse as it had been on 13 July. It was more like the rattle in the throat of an old woman who is about to go into the bathroom to do her dawn ablutions. I expected he had come to offer condolences on his death, and his voice was indeed crawling like a cripple as he assured me of his love.

"Forgive me, darling! You are the reason for everything. You only loved me because I lied to you. If I'd told you the truth you'd have rejected me outright from the beginning."

All he heard was my wailing, which had no end. I cried and cried, stricken with grief while he spoke, his voice a fragile whisper before he, too, broke down and wept.

"If you love me for who I really am, I am yours forever, whatever my name or my job or my status. If you loved the job and the name, that's something else."

"Why did you go to such lengths to deceive me? Why did you insist on humiliating me in public, in front of my family and relatives and friends?"

"I love you, my Munira. I can't let you go. I was going to tell you the truth when we were together, when I was yours and you were mine. But fate was faster. Listen, now you're my wife. I am prepared to do anything for you, do anything you want. But let's run away from this place, from my family and your family, from the people, the city. Let's live somewhere else, with this great love we have."

How could I live with a person who had deployed such skillful deception for a whole six months? How could I stab my family in the back so readily when I was the one accused of deceiving them?

The telephone receiver in its bear's-paw covering did not exude warmth as it had done on 13 July. It was cold and hard, and the little brown bear around it was either asleep or dead. Ali's voice receded and there was utter silence. I stood reeling in front of the large mirror on the wall and stared into it for a while. I saw the bride standing naively in her dress. That was the most difficult moment, as I undid the buttons one by one in an effort to assuage the pain. I threw the embroidered bodice on the floor and took off the diaphanous chiffon dress and stamped on it hysterically. Then I threw myself on the bed and howled uncontrollably until Mona and Nura came in. They were in a state of shock. Mona held me in her arms to comfort me while Nura ran her fingers through my hair, which I had undone and now hung sad and unkempt. Nura placed the sedative in my mouth while her other hand lifted the glass of water to my lips. Then they went out of the room. I stood naked under the tingling water of the shower, which began to wash away my tragedy, and massaged my eyes until they became drowsy. I wrapped the towel around me and went and lay down on the bed, languishing in the light that poured through the window, for the city had stopped wailing now and no more warnings echoed through its sky. No need for curfews anymore.

I thought for a moment as I prepared my pen to record the tragedy: how can the bottle of secrets hold all this sadness without exploding and shattering into fragments? Poor bottle, container of my secrets, my scraps of paper, all my sadnesses.

37

I stand accused of witchcraft!

He arrived in court before me and leveled the charges.
He claimed that I was a wife withheld from him by her
family's wish. He said that he had fallen ill as a result of a
spell cast on a glass of pomegranate juice I had served him.
He maintained that an Egyptian woman who worked at the
Center helped me weave the magic and, as a result, he stood
outside the gate of our house for hours on end, night and day.
In his deposition he stated that when I kissed him on the lips
I would tug forcibly at his hair and that I had pulled out some
hairs, which the Egyptian employee had used to perform a
binding spell that had made him obsessed with me. He also
said that when he visited me at home and I sat next to him, I
would take his hand and place it on my thigh and that I would
flirt with him and stroke his fingers and put my long fingernails under his nails and scrape out something with his aura
in it in order to bewitch him so that he would spend his whole
life following me around like a gentle lamb.

He said in his deposition that he had neglected his home
and his father and his children, that he no longer cared about
his job, and that his salary was constantly being docked due
to his absences and negligence, because he was spending
all his time with me, either whispering to me down the telephone or driving me around the streets of the city, besotted
by my beauty. He said that he had begun to feel a pain in his
lower back and that he was often lethargic and drowsy. There
wasn't a hospital or back pain clinic that he hadn't visited, but

all to no avail: the results of the x-rays and tests showed him to be completely healthy.

"Every time I close my eyes, your Honor, to go to sleep, I see hair and cord twisted together, tied in small knots."

He wept in court as he spoke to the sheikh, and sobbed and sighed as he related the events of his past life. He turned toward the tall windows of the chamber in a daze, his eyes staring, shining, fearful, like the eyes of one bewitched.

"I used to love my family, your Honor. Then I began to hate them all, hate the house. Even my father, I began to hate him."

No one interrupted him in front of the sheikh, who listened intently and stroked his thick beard.

"I would start the car without realizing it and drive over to her house. I would go in the middle of the night without wanting to."

He let out a faint snivel and wiped away a tear with the edge of his ghutra, then looked over to me on the other side of the chamber, standing next to my brother Muhammad.

"There wasn't a thing I didn't try, your Honor," he mumbled. "They told me to use senna with ginger, tamarind, caraway, and lavender. I boiled them up together and drank the potion for days and days but it didn't make any difference."

"Why didn't you try the Quranic recitations against magic?" asked the sheikh, visibly moved.

"I did, your Honor! I stood at the doors of sheikhs and reciters for hours on end. But when I heard the recitations my condition would grow worse. Sometimes I would even have convulsions and become nauseated."

"What do you ask now of the defendant?"

"I ask that she comes back to me as my wife, which she is, or that she releases me from the spell and returns all the money I spent on her without realizing it."

There was a long silence during which Ibn al-Asi stared at the tiles beneath his feet. Finally the judge cleared his throat and turned to me.

"What do you have to say in response to the words of the plaintiff?" he asked.

"All lies!"

"You did not put a spell on him?"

"Never. Neither my religion nor my upbringing would permit me to do such a thing. I am an educated woman."

"What proof is there of your claim?"

"Your Honor, what proof is there of his accusation?" asked my brother Muhammad.

The sheikh instructed him to remain silent as long as the defendant was present and capable of speaking.

"First, I demand that he provides evidence to back up what he is saying; otherwise it should be considered slander," I said. "Second, if I did put a spell on him to make him love me, I'd want to stay married to him and I'd agree to go with him!"

"But your Honor . . . ," he began.

"Silence!" interrupted the sheikh, and looked back at me.

"Does this mean that you are refusing to go with him as his wife?"

"Yes. I refuse categorically."

"Why has she bewitched you if she doesn't want to go with you as your wife?"

"She bewitched me when I was single and had a good job. Now that she knows about my marriage and children she's rejected me and left me bewitched."

"Do you still love her and want her?"

"Very much. And I'm ready to do everything she wants."

"And you? What do you say?"

"I refuse."

"But did you love him?"

"I did. But now I refuse him. I hate him."

Suddenly he stood up and ran toward me, throwing his body against me as he stooped to kiss my feet, asking me to forgive him for the things he had done because he had been unable to exercise his will. His crying echoed through the chamber as he pleaded with me to be his wife forever. My brother Muhammad and the policeman standing at the door dragged him back to his seat while the judge, clearly affected by the sight of a man prostrating himself at a woman's feet, lowered his head for a few seconds to take it all in. He then suggested that we be left alone together in order to carry on the discussion with greater freedom.

Al-Asi came over to me and tried to take my hand and kiss it. I told him sternly to stay where he was or I would walk out of the chamber as well. He said lots of things mixed with tears and sobs, and I cried too. I was not crying out of sympathy for his condition though, but for my own sorry state, his accusations of withcraft, his multiple deceptions. I spoke to him for a long time. I told him I would never marry a charlatan, an actor and a hypocrite, even if it meant spending my whole life without a husband or a son.

38

Look for your hair, ya Ibn al-Asi, and the stuff from under your fingernails. Rake through the earth and plunge the depths of the seas in search of bodily residues bearing your essence!

As I write my recollections today, I am sadder and more despondent than ever. I dream that when the bottle fills up with the tragedies Grandmother predicted would befall me the day she gave it to me, I take it to Half Moon Beach, where seagulls drenched in the oil and devastation of the Gulf War flounder and die. I throw the bottle far out to sea, unconcerned that the blackness of my tragedies will pollute the azure waters. Hasn't the oil killed the creatures of the sea before my ink? Perhaps I have brought those creatures back to life with my sad stories. Didn't Grandmother say that sad stories make the grass grow? Perhaps the sea creatures will rise from the dead when they read them.

Just before noon in court I saw Ibn al-Asi for the person he really was, his cajoling and conniving personality, his belief in superstition, magic, and nonsense. Hypocrite, weeping at my feet in the chamber, asking me to release him from the binding spell I'd put on him. As we drove home along roads crowded with taxis and Asian workers I thought about Mirvat, the Egyptian secretary at the Center. Once, inadvertently, I had told him that she read palms and chatted to the unmarried women about their fortunes and the husbands who awaited them. He began to ask about her regularly and wondered if she might be able to deflect a spell his cousin wanted to put on him. I didn't think much of it at the time, and asked him to think rationally and not be taken in by such superstition. Now, ya Hassan al-Asi, you can go to Hell! You can search heaven and earth for the hairs off your head that have been tied in knots and concealed. Look for them inside the bottle, the bottle with the tight cork cast into the depths of the Nile. Go there and hire boats and divers, search the whole of the Nile so you can find the bottle and your hair inside it; then burn it and cast the fragile ashes of your love for me along the banks of that mighty river.

I wonder if he'll go on long journeys, wandering through the Empty Quarter, roaming the deserts of al-Summan, searching acacia trees and camel's thorn, rummaging through rimth bushes and untouched dunes. Will he dig in the sand and scratch at the roots of the ghada, looking for his precious little hairs so he can burn them and undo the spell? Will he hunt down all the reptiles and tiny insects and cut them open in case something bearing his aura is in their bowels? Will he butcher the desert wolves and hyenas? Will his rifle tear the harvest birds and turtledoves to shreds?

I can see him in pursuit of a lizard as it runs terrified toward its lair. He leaps on its back and grabs its spiny tail, and as he unsheathes his sharp knife, he notices on the yellow skin of its belly the scar of a surgical operation. "The spell that binds me is here," he says to himself, "inside the belly of this lizard, ya Ibnat al-Sahi!" Then he scatters its innards with a quick thrust of his keen blade, and fumbles through the half-digested remnants of the plants and insects the creature has gathered from the desert floor. He spots something wrapped and knotted. It emits a disgusting smell. He picks it up, hurling his victor's cry across the Nafud desert. "Yes! I have found the spell. I have found the magic here!" He burns it in a frenzy of delirium and returns to the city, certain of his victory, until the moment I reawake his longing for my eyes and he whispers to himself, "The spell I burned in the belly of the lizard was put on someone else!"

I remember the sister of the corpse washer who washed and perfumed my grandmother's body, the woman who could not see the Kaaba as she walked around it, whose son could not bury her since no grave or tomb would receive her. I remember how she placed things into women's coffins, little pouches fastened tightly with cord, and left them there to decompose with the corpse, consigned to the grave forever. Go, ya Ibn al-Asi, to the cemeteries. Dig up the graves one by one and look through the bones of the dead for your hair and nail clippings, then burn them. Perhaps eventually you'll burn your false love and your counterfeit feelings.

And Lillian, damn her! What on earth possessed her to make you that pomegranate juice? Your filthy mouth didn't deserve it. Damn my hand, for I forced you to sip the juice while I held the glass, thinking that I would celebrate your return from Kuwait after you had led the mission to find the important missing person. I remember wondering then why you refused to drink it. You said you had a sore throat, that it was swollen and you had a virus. I never imagined that the birds of sorcery and superstition were nesting in your stupid head.

But you weren't stupid, were you, ya Ibn al-Dahhal? I was the stupid one. I really was a stupid, clumsy, naive woman. I was the one bewitched, my sight and intuition the ones obscured. Your scheming, your little conspiracies, they wouldn't have fooled a teenage girl, like Fatima al-Hasawiya, who discovered the identity of Mueed on their first encounter. I saw you every day, sat next to you every day in the different cars you hired. You were so careless you even let me get into my own brother's car, but I didn't notice. You couldn't even be bothered to change the inside. You left the plastic bird dangling from the rearview mirror. Were you throwing ashes in my face so that I would be blinded and see only you, like the ruler of Iraq beguiled us with his chemical weapons? Were all those lies you told, all those facts you distorted, a result of my magic—just as the ruler of Iraq fell under the spell of Kuwait, seduced by her oil, asserting that she was the nineteenth province of Iraq? Had he gone there with his tanks and armored cars to burn the oil wells that the enchantress Kuwait had used to bind his heart to her? And you, ya al-Dahhal, did you drive the armored vehicle of your treachery toward me, not aware of what you were doing, hopelessly under the influence of Mirvat's spell?

Poor Mirvat! She grazes obliviously in the corridors of the Remand Center, picking up leftovers like a stray animal, never missing a piece of chicken or a slice of fried fish. She provides a range of catering services for the women who work there, from complete banquets for special occasions to a simple Turkish coffee and a quick read of the grains in the bottom of the cup. She pays no attention to the sarcastic winks they exchange as she focuses her concentration on the dark brown sludge, the patterns and swirls left against the white porcelain. The way to happiness is open, she confirms, as she points into the cup with her index finger so wide in fact that good fortune will be coming soon. Some of them hold out their palms coyly, and allow her to inform them where the lines are headed: the love line, the life line, the happiness line. She possesses an extraordinary talent, which is revealed the moment she takes the extended palm in her own. "No, no, no, Allaaah. It can't be true! It's absolutely wonderful, really!" Mirvat offers memorable and exciting promises and the expressions on their faces shift from amazement to fear to hope, accompanied by much frowning and beaming. Then

184

Mirvat assures the one whose palm lies in her hand that love is not far away and that all she has to do is to put her trust in her relatives and those around her and she will have a long and happy life.

39

By the time the judge and my brother returned, a stony silence had settled on the chamber. Muhammad shot me a vicious look. I'd been alone with Hassan al-Asi for almost twenty minutes. He had protested before he went out, refusing to leave me alone with a strange man, maintaining to the judge that such a situation was in violation of the sharia on the pretext that I was the wife of Ali al-Dahhal, whereas the person before us was Hassan al-Asi.

The judge cleared his throat and wiped his glasses with the edge of his shmagh before placing them on his nose and looking around the chamber, first at us, then at al-Asi, and finally through the tall windows at the high walls in the distance. He cast a glance at the clerk by his side and whispered some instructions before finally addressing Ibn al-Asi.

"Have you reached a solution?"

"I don't think so."

"Well, have you determined exactly what it is you want?"

"My wife returns to me or she gives me back the money I spent on her."

"So, will you return to him?" he asked as he looked at me under his glasses.

"No. Never. I demand that he divorces me."

"Didn't you agree to take this man as your husband?"

"Yes I did."

"Well then, he still wants you."

"But he lied to me. He even made up his feelings."

"But you don't know what his feelings really were."

"He forged his ID card and lied about his job and family for months! After all that, it's not difficult for him to make up feelings."

"But you wanted him as he was, as he appeared in front of you. What does it matter about his name or his job?"

"That's all very well, but how can you build a marriage on lies and deceit?"

"Your final decision then?"

"I want a divorce."

"And what do you say?"

"I demand the whole of the bride price, and all the gifts I gave her."

"But he didn't pay a dowry, not a single riyal, your Honor!" I shouted.

"Be quiet!" The judge raised his hand then added, "The marriage contract is here in front of me, signed by the ma'dhun and two witnesses. It states that he paid sixty thousand riyals."

"He promised he'd bring it to my father but he never did."

The birds stopped chirping on the window ledges outside the courtroom. All I could hear was muttering and babbling; all I could see were scowling faces, mouths opening and closing in agitation, and hands gesticulating wildly. Outside, the square in front of the courthouse was heaving with Asian workers and toothpick sellers and petition writers. The signs of the lawyers' offices seemed to sway blackly before my eyes as if they were about to plummet from the painted, peeling façades of the buildings. On one of the balconies overlooking the square, an Egyptian woman in a hijab appeared and hung out her laundry on a limp washing line.

I was crossing the road next to my brother and a motorbike almost snatched away my abaya, which had turned into a black balloon, bloated by the wind. I don't know how but I saw myself rising up into the air in the inflated abaya like a zeppelin, rising little by little until I was on a level with the tops of the buildings, and then floating above them. I could see the roof of the courthouse, full of air-conditioning units and old tables and tattered leather chairs where people had once sat anxiously, dreaming of a justice that resembled the swollen balloon of my abaya. I drifted higher and saw the city and its streets sleeping silently, untroubled. The roofs of the houses were like hidden piazzas cut off from the world, crowded with secret things and tools and gadgets and pots and pans, each with an untold tale to tell. I moved higher and higher, and saw my sister Mona and my colleague Nabeela; I saw Fatima al-Hasawiya and Maytha al-Badawiya and drugged-up Hasna; I saw them the size of beans as they crossed the road with their abayas billowing in the wind. I saw them ascending gradually above the city until they reached me in the open sky. We flew side by side like witches on the wind but without wands in our long-nailed hands to wave at humankind and turn them into frogs or nibbling rats.

What about *my* fingers? Were the nails too long, like the nails of a genie or a witch? The judge had kept my brother back for a moment after I left the courtroom and instructed him that he should encourage me to cut my long nails. He had stared for some time at my fingers as they held the pen that signed my statement and an agreement to repay the fictitious sixty thousand riyals, which had been paid to me on paper only. The judge wasn't interested in my tragedy. He believed, and explained so to my brother, that the primary violation of Islam, the underlying Jahiliya, lay in my fingernails. My long heathen fingernails, which the judge had taken such an exception to, were the reason for the city's ruination. It was they that had deceived and tricked and lied and betrayed and

forged and stolen. My fingers with their long nails, they were ✓
the ones that had instigated the whole catastrophe.

They used to tell us that a woman's fingernails are part
of her beauty, and they said that with them she scratches the
face of the truth. As for me, I used mine to scratch the judge's
patience and his peace of mind. I scratched the silence of the
city, its certainty and tranquility. I scratched the submissive-
ness of obscure and unknown women. And if it were in my
power to hold the witch's wand between my long-nailed fingers, I would; and I would rap it against the head of Hassan
al-Asi and mutter the unintelligible words of my spell and
turn him into an ass and spirit him to a dusty back street for
the kids and young guys to have some fun with.

I'd saved up thirty-six thousand riyals since I'd started
work. My father helped me out with the rest so that I could
pay the full sum to Mr. al-Asi, the oppressor and oppressed,
in order for him to release me from his clutches and hand me
the deed to my freedom.

40

O n this day, Monday the twelfth of Rabi' al-Thani 1412, there did appear before me, Ibn Wasea, Judge at the High Court in Riyadh, Hassan bin Asi, whose identity is duly recorded in the court register, and who made claim against Hamad al-Sahi, also attending.

In his deposition, Mr. al-Asi reported the following: "The defendant married his daughter Munira to me in the month of Shaaban while he was a patient in the general medical hospital in exchange for a dowry of sixty thousand riyals, which I delivered to him in his hand. Then the woman put a spell on me with the assistance of an Egyptian woman employed in her place of work, with the result that I no longer knew anything of myself save that I gave her money and jewels far above what is normal, to a value greater than two hundred thousand riyals. He then pretended not to know who I was and showed me a marriage contract which named the husband as Ali al-Dahhal. Now I demand that he turns over my wife to me or he returns the money I have spent on his daughter. This is my claim."

When asked about this, the defendant replied, "The plaintiff came to me and asked for my daughter Munira's hand. He said his name was Ali bin Fahd al-Dahhal and that he was a major in the military and that he was extremely busy all of the time. I requested some time to ask after him. When I inquired, I was told that the family was reputable and well-known. However, when I went to his place of work I was unable to meet him so I did not get acquainted with him there. When

I informed him of this he told me that he had to undertake many special duties and often people did not know where he was. When I went into hospital for medical treatment, he came to me there a number of times and asked me to give over my daughter to him. I told him to bring Sheikh Ibn Saleh, as that gentleman is known to me. The next thing I knew, he appeared with a registrar I didn't know and two witnesses I had never seen before; but because of his insistence I married my daughter to him with this ma'dhun and we all signed— myself, he, and the two soldiers he had brought as witnesses. When I returned home, he came to me the same night with the ma'dhun and asked me how much I wanted as a dowry. After some discussion we agreed on sixty thousand, not including the expenses of the engagement present and the wedding. My daughter signed the agreement that night. However I did not receive from him that night any money, having been assured by him that he would bring it later. He did present my daughter with a ring and a gift of diamond jewelry but they did not consummate the marriage. Later on, one of my relatives told me that this man was called Hassan and not Ali, and that was when the problem occurred. If the plaintiff has proven that he handed me the money and has sworn an oath to that effect, then I have no objection to paying him but I am not prepared to give him my daughter."

When Mr. al-Sahi's daughter was questioned she replied, "I first got to know him as so-and-so and if I had known his name was so-and-so I would not have agreed to marry him. All I received from him was the engagement present and various gifts that he used to bring of his own volition as an expression of his love for me and his desire to marry me. He told me that his father had passed away and that his mother was in mourning and could not come to meet me. So until his mother felt better he brought his aunt to see me and to ask if

191

I would marry him. But in fact his father was still alive and the woman who came to our house was not related to him in any way."

The plaintiff maintained that this entire story was concocted and that he had no idea about it. He continued, "What benefit would accrue to me by recording a name other than my own on the marriage contract, and what would become of any children I had from her if they did not bear my true name? Perhaps it was under the influence of the spell she cast, for I did things that I was not aware of."

The defendant said that she was totally prepared to return everything she had been given by the plaintiff. As for the magic, she said, that was just a ploy he had stooped to, and if she had done that, she asked, then why would she want a divorce from him? For this reason each one of them was asked to take the legal oath as each was sticking to their story. After the oath, however, the plaintiff said, "I will not divorce her until she releases me from the spell she has put on me." After further discussion on the matter the two sides agreed on the payment of the sum of sixty thousand riyals, whereupon the session was adjourned on the understanding that the amount would be delivered at a subsequent session. The two parties attended the subsequent session and the plaintiff was handed the amount in a check signed by the woman, Munira. But the defendant refused once again to divorce her until he was released from her magic spell. A discussion took place with him requesting that he end the case without further delay according to what had previously been agreed. This was in the presence of the ma'dhun who had conducted the marriage ceremony at the hospital but who, when asked, failed to remember the person or his appearance, recalling simply that he was in a hurry to complete the ceremony and that her father was undergoing medical treatment in hospital and that none of her family attended. The couple were then brought together one final time in private and asked if they still wished to separate. The woman was adamant that she wanted to end all connection to the defendant. As for the plaintiff, he continued to procrastinate on the grounds that the magic was still rendering him incapable of controlling his actions, and that he wanted her to be his wife and would not divorce her. We urged the plaintiff, in the presence of the woman's guardian and the lawyer assigned to him, to consider the military and security implications of the case, whereupon the plaintiff pleaded with the woman to accept him as her husband and forgive him. She did, however, reject the proposal most vehemently, which renders null and void his accusation that she has used magic against him. Thus the judge pronounced her divorced without incidence of unlawful seclusion or the consummation of the marriage. According to the evidence presented, the police did not apprehend any person by the name of Ali al-Dahhal bearing an identification card with the same number and date of birth as the one found in the possession of the plaintiff. Furthermore, as the number and date of birth attributed to this Ali al-Dahhal have no basis in truth, the case is closed with the divorce agreement herein described. As for the aforementioned marriage contract, it is annulled. Thus have I ruled and ordered, having instructed the defendant not to remarry until after the decree is ratified, for in her case there is no waiting period since the marriage was not consummated.

Submitted on the twelfth day of Jumada al-Thaniya 1412, may God's praise be upon our Prophet Muhammad and upon his clan and upon the entirety of his companions.

When Munira had read the decree of her deliverance, every word of which was a missile, every letter a stone, she folded it with both her hands and let out a long, deep sigh.

She looked up at the ceiling for the spider that always stood at the edge of the plaster in readiness to run down its prey, grab it with its pincers, and munch it quietly and calmly between its mandibles. Munira would swear to her friend Nabeela that she could see the spider's teeth as it devoured its prey, a lost gnat or a stray fly, and she insisted that the spider wiped its mouth after completing its daily meal. She would swear also that she saw the spider's sated face smiling gormlessly as it retraced its steps back across the ceiling to its home that hung limp and quivering in the corner of the room. I am like the naive gnat, she thought. I fell into the trap of Hassan al-Asi, whose clean teeth never stopped grinning.

Oh, Nabeela. I burst into tears every time I think about those teeth that nibbled my mouth and frivolously chewed my lips but didn't mean it, while I gave myself to him like the sacrificial gnat. How could I, at my age, with my mind and my experience, fall such easy prey to an idiot like that? But then was it he who was the idiot or was it I? He conspired with the woman who said she was his aunt, and the waiter at Maxime's, and the ma'dhun, and the two soldiers he brought as witnesses. I simply conspired against myself and walked blind and trusting behind him. I must have been insane. And all the while fate led me on, shielding from my eyes all evidence that could have pointed to his conspiracy.

41

Everything is written. It's true what my mother says, and it brings her peace of mind: "What's written on the forehead the eye shall surely see." It was written that my brother should travel to Britain on a training course. It was written that my brother Muhammad should become too preoccupied with his business in scented woods and honey to look out for us. It was written that my mother and brother Saad and sister Mona should go out on the evening of the thirteenth of July last year. It was written that I should still have to write the important analysis of my master's dissertation and decide to stay home and finish the research rather than go to Hardee's with them. It was written that I should pick up the phone when it rang so insistently in order that the chemistry of my heart could collide with the rich tapestry of his voice. It was written that he would seduce me by following my weekly column "Rose in a Vase" until I became immersed in conversation with him, and the words changed to sighs and gasps and plain, unadulterated flirtation. It was written that when I saw him for the first time, his beautiful eyes would cocoon themselves in my vulnerable and deprived heart. It was written that my father would go to visit him at his work and stand at the real Major al-Dahhal's door for a few minutes without managing to see him, inches away from exposing the whole affair, and then turn around and leave. It was written that I would change my mind every time I thought about calling my old college friend, Sarah al-Dahhal, to ask her about him, putting the receiver back down before dialing, or hanging up when her younger brother answered and then went off to fetch her. It was written that I would sit next to him in my brother's car and not notice the plastic bird as it swung from side to side with the swaying motion of the Caprice. It was written that I would write a letter to my brother, Major Saleh, in Britain informing him that I'd gotten engaged to a young major and that I'd be getting married soon, and was really sorry that we weren't delaying the wedding until he returned. It was written that I would put a photo of the groom in the envelope, but then forget about the letter and never send it. If he had received it, he would have seen the photograph of the private who stood outside his office door for hours on end like a guard dog, and recognized him and told us from over there in Britain what was going on. It was written that I would not learn from the tragedies I observed. I ignored the signs and warnings in Fatima al-Hasawiya, who discovered that Bandar was just the operating name for Mr. Mueed. Why didn't I realize that Ali al-Dahhal was the assumed name of Mr. Hassan al-Asi during all those months I spent with him?

It was written that I would drag my body around the corridors of the court building, in front of prosecution boards and the voice investigation agency. He had made tape recordings of many of our phone calls in an attempt to prove that I dabbled in magic. In each call he would ask me about the Egyptian woman, Mirvat, who worked at the Center, and how she read palms and coffee cups, asking if I could get her to read his palm for him. Then he would complain about his cousin who was crazy about him and how she had conspired with a witch to put a spell on him so that he would fall in love with her and marry her. It was written that he would edit together, craftily and with great skill, sentences to prove I was working magic. It was written that the Leader in Baghdad would attack Kuwait and enable al-Asi to hide every secret and situation behind the circumstances of the war, and that I would have no right to ask him where he disappeared to, or ask anyone else about him, because both he and I were being watched. It was written that Jordan would be against the foreign presence in the region, and that the supervisor of my dissertation, Dr. Yasser Shaheen, would be deported. It was written that my studies for the Master's should grind to a halt and that my research should switch from investigating adolescent behavior in young girls to observing the behavior of spiders on the ceiling of my room. It was written that our Filipina maid would know the face of Ibn al-Asi from the years of his bringing the daily papers from my brother's office to our house, and then see him entering our house as my fiancé and say nothing because she thought we knew. It was written that none of Ibn al-Asi's many visits to our house ever coincided with the presence of my cousin Nasir who knew that he was just a poor private who deserved compassion and charity. It was written that my brother Saleh would provoke him by pushing his foot into his chest and knocking him over on his back when he asked if he was related to the journalist Munira al-Sahi. That blow kindled a burning desire in Ibn al-Asi's breast to avenge his honor, which had slumbered for many years, and caused him to wreak revenge as if he were some major player in an underworld turf war. It was also written that I would not understand what the Arabs understand: the bad omen of seeing something unexpected prior to embarking on a journey or a raid. I didn't pay attention to the secret of the little insect that withdrew slowly under my pillow immediately after I had put the bear's-paw phone down, having just chatted to Ibn al-Asi for almost an hour.

All the time I kept writing on pieces of paper decorated with flowers, and it was as if the flowers grew with the sad stories. And as I wrote, I felt that the words were like stones

197

that I hurled at my foolish self, and when the words wouldn't express, I began to doodle on the edges of the flowered paper. I drew tears falling out of nowhere. I drew my wide eyes that had led me to ruin. I drew round shapes and stars and crowns and military boots and thick beards and spectacles, and English letters and full lips with a neat mustache above them. I drew and drew until I was tired, then closed the notepad, placing the pen, with the thread carefully wrapped around it and three cheap pearl beads attached to the end, inside.

After the words dried up and the doodles died in my hand, I got up and closed the curtains patterned with huge roses, took off my clothes, and put on a short silk nightie. I undid my hair and let it fall over my shoulders, switched on the bedside lamp, and turned up the stereo. Out flowed the voice of Muhammad Abdu, whom I love to distraction:

Oooooh, my heart burns for you,
Can't stand a night without you
You and those big wide eyes
No one else but you will do.

In the gloomy dressing table mirror I see the shape of a woman dancing quietly, her body arching like a sad and hungry feline. Her firm figure sways from side to side, and tears flow incessantly from her eyes. Every now and again she lifts up her hands, pushes back her thick hair, and shakes her head like a wild filly as she sniffs to deter her swelling tears. Then she raises a crumpled handkerchief clutched in her left hand to mop up an unruly teardrop about to flow from the corner of her eye. Come here, Munira of the mirror. Hold me a while and soothe my troubled soul so that I can sleep. Come and share my bed, for no one else can hold me after today.

The thrombosis will finish off Father and the same red GMC that bore my grandmother before will take him to the graveyard. My mother will withdraw into herself, sad and alone. My brother Saleh will return to his work, and will appoint another private to run his errands, as if everything that has happened means nothing to him. My brother Muhammad will see to his chain of shops that sell honey and incense and perfume and clothes and Islamic audiocassettes, and he will call them the Sheikh Muhammad al-Sahi Group Limited. My elder sister Nura will drool after her husband like a house cat, and hug her little ones apprehensively. And my little sister Mona: she might marry an extremely handsome and cultured young man and have a son after two years of inner turmoil, having discovered that her husband suffered from psychological scars because he had been sexually abused as a child. What a fate that would be, Mona!

42

As for me, the days will blow me a sweet wind, as the horoscope always says. My brother Muhammad, with his long beard, will scream at my father as he lay dying. The red shmagh he perfumes with scented oil will keep sliding down the back of his head, and he will reposition it every time with an angry and trembling hand. His saliva will fly in my father's face, and his fierce looks will fall like whiplashes on my mother's silence. "If she's not been touched, she should accept the first man who asks for her. If she has preserved her honor, let her prove it and marry the first person who knocks on the door." And in the thick of his fury he will point to the front door.

The days will pass in slow monotony. An acquaintance of my father's from the incense and carpet souk will appear, bringing with him my bride price and his sixty years. He will take me away as expressions of consolation from those around me ring in my ears, "Anyway you're a spinster now. You're over thirty!" I will convince myself that they are right and go to live in a new villa in the exclusive al-Nakheel district. He will provide me with a Filipino driver and a new Lexus. I will wait for him three consecutive nights while he visits his other three wives, and on the fourth night I will tell him stories, but not stories from the bottle. I will make up stories, as if he is my Shahriyar, not so that he will sheath his sword and refrain from killing me, but to sharpen his blunted weapon and quench my burning thirty-year-old's desire before he dozes off and his snoring wakes the city. I will cry when I am alone, having heard the whispers of those around me, "He really spoils her. She wants for nothing." I want for nothing. I will give birth to a daughter, who will fill my loneliness and free time. I will write down everything that has happened to me, and what will happen. I will write down what I have dreamed and what I will dream. I will see a slim young man, who has studied interior design in Italy, in the home décor shop. He will come to my villa after I have been married three years in order to put amazing touches of beauty to my walls. He will add his magic touch to the walls of my body, rekindle its enchantment and reawaken its wonder. My walls will shine with the strokes of his wonderful brush; I will plunge into his depths completely, and he will plunge mine. I will spend three nights in a row with him and on the fourth I will lie down by the side of my sixty-year-old husband. In the morning I will weep as I feel guilt chewing my fingers. The young man will justify to me my guilt in the name of love, in the name of desire, and he will introduce me to European Renaissance art. He will cover the walls of the sitting room with copies of oil paintings: this one is *The Harvest* by Van Gogh, this is *Fish Magic* by Paul Klee, that one is a picture of a woman sitting on the beach by Pablo Picasso, and that one, which he will hang over the women's entrance, is a painting by an artist called Klimt. I will be very happy that I have found someone to trust, but the inner pain of my infidelity, which will eventually destroy my beauty, will not cease. It will disappear, though, as soon as I see the interior decorator's eyes and I kiss them all night long on the bed in my other room. That's the room I will suggest to my sixty-year-old husband I should sleep in during the three nights when I am alone, so that I don't remember him and smell the scent of perfume from his clothes. My lover will decorate the walls of my new room with gentle lemon wallpaper and we will put the twenty-nine-inch television in it and a video player, and we will stay up every night and watch a new film, and end up on the soft, cozy bed, with luxurious sheets and pillows from America.

I will get a good job, with more than forty women working under me. In the summer, my husband will travel to Morocco and Cairo on the pretext of tests and medical treatment. I will not be allowed to travel abroad without a mahram, or without my guardian's permission. I will go alone with a forged consent form, signed by my lover, who has perfected my sixty-year-old husband's signature. We will travel together for one marvellous week to Marbella in Spain. I will leave my daughter with my mother and my sister Mona. The following year we will visit Italy and I will see the university where he studied interior design for five years. We will visit the area where he lived. I will get to know lots of museums. This time I will come back and find that my mother has gone into a coma. I will cry a lot and push my face against the window of the intensive care unit. I will cry for my mother, and because I left without hearing her voice and embracing her. I will embrace my brother Saad and weep for hours and hours. How painful it feels now to remember putting my arm around my lover's waist in the streets of Rome, and kissing him in front of every statue in every piazza while my lonely mother was collapsing in front of my sister Mona and my little daughter. I will apologize to my lover politely, and I will ignore his repeated calls, and I will withdraw from him gradually. I will join a Quran memorization class in al-Andalus Mosque next to my house. I will become an active young woman once again. I will tour different areas and give talks to deviant girls. I will hand out Islamic audiocassettes. I will wear black gloves on my hands and black socks on my feet and I will put the niqab over my face. My brother Muhammad will stand by my side, joyful and enthusiastic. I will deliver lectures on the materialism of European societies and their moral decay. I will remove the paintings by the infidel artists from my house and hang up Quranic verses in their place. I will try to guide my stray sister Mona on to the straight and narrow but I will fail many times. I will stop when she attacks me derisively and reveals that she knew about my relationship with the interior designer, and that he had been abroad with me more than once. She will attend a modern art course at the Sheffield Institute and follow that with a course in ceramics. She will learn how to paint murals and will sign contracts with a number of interior design companies. Her gift of designing ceramics on walls will spread far and wide. One day he will see her name: Mona al-Sahi. He will call her with the excuse of a contract for some work on a new palace. He will meet her on the site. Then he will learn that she is divorced and lives alone in a large mansion, and that she only has one son, who is six years old. He will discover that she is my sister. He will take his revenge on me by having a passionate relationship with her. Even though my sister Mona will try to hide it, her shining eyes will give her away as they glow with deep love. One day I will say to her, "Even though you're hiding from me the fact that you're doing something wrong, your eyes give you away." Then I will suggest that she marry her mystery man, to protect herself and put her conscience at rest. She will cry so inconsolably that I am surprised but she will not tell me anything.

I will open my eyes one morning and look for my sixty-year-old husband. He hasn't shown up for almost a week, and I haven't asked after him at his other three houses. I will ignore the matter while I look for the bottle in which I have collected what I have started to call scandals, but which I once called tragedies. Now I see it as a bottle of depravity. I will decide to get rid of it but I will find no trace of it. I will scream at the Indonesian maid as I walk, horrified, down the stairs of my mansion, but she will reply that she doesn't know what I am talking about. I will search high and low but I will not find the bottle anywhere, and my sixty-year-old husband will not return. I will imagine that he has discovered the antique bottle with the faded Indian symbols upon it, and is trembling, thinking it is the container of a magic spell cast to attach him to me and separate him from his three wives. He will try to take some of the pieces of paper out of the narrow mouth of the bottle, but to no avail. He will decide to smash the bottle, not knowing how I wept when I was a child and refused to free the wild chafer that was trapped inside the bottle by breaking it. The shards of glass will fly all over his car and he will read my life story, my defeats, my being deceived, my divorce, my relationship with the interior designer. He in his turn will weep at having fallen victim to such deceit. He will try to remember our first night, whether I was a virgin or not. He will decide to watch me from the corner of the street, concealed in a rented car, and he will look around the home décor shops for a young man who studied in Italy. He will acquire a small revolver. He will make up his mind . . . .

"Good God! What an awful life," said Munira al-Sahi as she imagined her future. She turned off the stereo, pulled the curtains open, and looked down at the red GMC parked in the quiet street below. No sooner had she returned to sit on the edge of the bed, in her very short nightdress, than she heard the pigeons cooing on the window ledge outside, tapping the glass with their beaks.

43

In the silent days that followed Desert Storm, Munira al-Sahi thought constantly about the previous months as she watched the plaster rim of the hung ceiling, waiting for a spider to come crawling along, trundling indolently toward its prey. But for days and nights she didn't see a thing, so one cold evening she leaned her slender frame over the banister and shouted down to the Filipina maid Lillian.

Lillian moved around the edges of the room on the small aluminum stepladder, climbing up with her feather duster and inserting it into the gap between the edge of the ceiling and the wall and giving it a quick shake. Every so often she checked the feathers to see if a spider was attached to them, but found nothing. Munira ordered her servant to come down and took over herself. She climbed up the stepladder and arched her neck as she tried to peer into the gap, but she was unable to locate the insect that had nonchalantly traversed her pillow that evening in the middle of last July.

When she was once again alone in the room, Munira locked the door and lit a yellow scented candle. The furniture jerked in the flickering light. She stood up slowly and opened the rose-patterned curtains and looked out at the red sky and the blazing ball of fire as it dipped toward the horizon. She spotted two cats playing affectionately on top of the garden wall. They jumped onto the roof of the car. She noticed how the male cat tried to control his female by biting her neck while he positioned his backside above her in a well-practiced manner before finally inserting himself inside her. Suddenly a screech from the female shattered the twilight silence and she shot out from beneath the tom and disappeared under the car. Munira's heart thumped indignantly and her face turned black with anger. She picked up a small green glass elephant off her bedside cabinet and ran back to the window, roaring furiously. She slammed open the aluminum window, slid back the mosquito screen and looked for the two philandering cats, but the yard was completely empty. Then suddenly she spotted the male sniffing underneath the female's tail and she hurled the little elephant ornament at it. Fragments of glass flew in all directions as the ornament smashed into the tiles and the two cats sped off toward the gate. Munira slumped down in the corner of the room. Her body shook as she wept, sweat poured from her neck and forehead, and she cracked her slender fingers as waves of desolation overwhelmed her.

After she had calmed down a little, Munira al-Sahi opened the dressing table drawer, took out a bottle of old perfume, and sprayed some on her neck. As she placed it back in the drawer she noticed a piece of folded paper. It was the divorce document. She removed it, contemplated it for a moment in the light of the scented candle, and began to read it again for the thousand and first time, until she reached the bit that said: *The plaintiff maintained that this entire story was concocted and that he had no idea about it. He continued, "What benefit would accrue to me by recording a name other than my own on the marriage contract, and what would become of any children I had from her if they did not bear my true name? Perhaps it was under the influence of the spell she cast, for I would do things that I was not aware of."*

As Munira read these words she reached furiously into the drawer, feeling for a pair of scissors. She remembered the scissors in the story of the woodcutter who abandoned his three daughters in the desert and cut the edge off his shmagh so that his youngest daughter would sleep on soundly in his scent, not noticing that he had left. She remembered the story well. It was the one for which she had won the bottle of secrets and sad stories. She continued the search but to no avail, and finally she found herself drawn to the small flickering flame. The edge of the document was almost touching the fire. Seconds later the flame began to grow and pungent black smoke rose up the side of the paper. The twisted black ashes of the words began to fall on to the marble floor of the room. Hassan al-Asi fell, followed by her father, Hamad al-Sahi, and then the judge. And despite her hand trembling as the fire approached her own name, she did not flinch, but made sure that the candle's flame devoured the whole of the document even though the heat burned her forefinger and thumb, until finally she threw down the last tiny, unburned piece of paper.

Breathing deeply she wiped the ashes into her palm with her fingers and threw them out of the window. Then she went into the bathroom and, despite the cold, took off her clothes. She turned the shower on full. The hot water gushed over her naked body, making its familiar sound, sweeping away her sadness as she mumbled something in the gloom that sounded like an old song by an unknown singer. As she sat in front of the dressing table wrapped in a thick bathrobe, she heard the voice of the muezzin cutting through the darkness. She wrapped her hair in a towel and closed the window tightly. Then she snuggled up under the thick woolen blanket on her bed and, to the sound of the pigeons cooing and tapping on the window, she sank into a deep sleep.

Glossary

1981: the year of the assault on the Kaaba, the Holy Sanctuary in Mecca, by a group of men led by Juhayman al-Utaybi. The subsequent siege of the Sanctuary lasted many days until the rebels were defeated. The incident had a profound effect on Saudi politics and society.

abaya: a long black garment worn by women over their clothes, covering them from neck to toe; can be baggy or tight fitting. There are a variety of styles and cuts and some are decorated or embroidered at the edges. Saudi women complement the **abaya** with a headscarf and full-face veil.

bin: son of, when occurring between names.

burka: a face covering.

Commission: The Commission for the Promotion of Virtue and the Prevention of Vice (CPVPV), the body of Muslim men that check adherence to true Islamic behavior; the so-called Religious Police.

Eid: either of the Islamic feasts—Eid al-Fitr, coming at the end of Ramadan, or Eid al-Adha, falling at the end of the Hajj, or pilgrimage.

fatwa: a religious edict, legally binding when issued by the senior **ulama** of the Kingdom.

ghada: a small bush that grows widely in central and Northern Saudi Arabia, and reaches a meter in height. Its wood is excellent for making fires and burns for a long time.

ghutra: a man's headcloth, made of fine white material. Like the **shmagh**, it is normally worn over a **tagiya**, or skullcap, and a black double band, or **i'gal**, is placed on top. There are a variety of styles in which the **ghutra** or **shmagh** can be arranged for formal and informal occasions, either allowing the edges to fall down over the shoulders or throwing them up over the top of the head.

haram: religiously forbidden or unlawful; taboo.

Hasawi: from the Region of **al-Hasa**, a large oasis to the southeast of Riyadh. **Hasawiya** a woman from **al-Hasa**.

hayy: the Bedouin encampment.

hijab: a headscarf that leaves the face uncovered.

Ibn: 'son of,' when used at the beginning of names.

Ibna(t): daughter of.

Ibn al-Mulawwah: Arab poet (died 688). His full name was Qays bin al-Mulawwah, celebrated for his passionate poems in honor of Layla, his beloved.

i'gal: black rings of cord worn on top of the **ghutra** or **shmagh.** Some Saudi men wear the **shmagh** or **ghutra** without the **i'gal**. This is seen as a sign of piety.

insha'allah: if God wills it.

Jahiliya: the period before Islam; the 'Age of Ignorance,' of non-Islam.

jihad: effort for the sake of God, sometimes referring to "Holy War." See **mujahid**.

Kaaba: The House of God, the stone structure at Mecca to which Muslims turn when they pray.

Kuthayr: Arab poet (died c.728), real name Abu Hamza al-Khuza'i al-Madani, also known as Kuthayr Azza, after the woman he loved and celebrated in his poetry.

la ilaha illa Allah: 'there is no god but God.'

ma'dhun: a religious cleric who, among other duties, officiates at the signing of marriage contracts.

mahram: a male guardian, a man whom a woman cannot marry, for example, her father or brother, and including her husband and sons if she is married.

majlis: a place where people sit and hold meetings; a room in a house for this purpose; or a tent set up temporarily.

masha'Allah: 'what God wills,' used to utter approval or as a counter against envy.

mishlah: ankle-length diaphanous cloak, normally black, dark brown, or cream, trimmed with gold braid, and worn by men over the **thobe** on formal and ceremonial occasions.

muezzin: the man who performs the call to prayer.

mufti: a senior religious figure, dispenser of a **fatwa**.

mujahid: (pl. mujahideen). In this context the men who volunteered to go and wage **jihad** against the Soviet occupation of Afghanistan.

Najdi: from **al-Najd**, central Saudi Arabia, where Riyadh is situated.

nashama: courageous ones, plural of **nushami**.

niqab: a full veil covering the entire face.

Nizar Qabbani: celebrated Syrian romantic poet (1923–98).

oud: a musical instrument, a lute.

qaroura: bottle. In Islamic and Arab culture, a bottle symbolizes woman. The Prophet Muhammad said "**rifqan bi-l-qaraweer**," meaning 'treat women kindly.'

rimth: desert bush used for kindling.

riyal: the Saudi unit of currency.

shabka: a gift of gold (usually necklace, bracelet, rings, and earrings) given by a man to his fiancée on the occasion of their engagement.

shafallah: a long-living bush with white or pink flowers and small edible berries.

shari'a: the body of Islamic law.

shawerma: meat or chicken cooked on a rotating vertical spit. Often the meat is tightly packed in conical form around the spit and rotates slowly to be carved off as it cooks. The carved strips of meat are placed in pita breads with salad, French fries, mayonnaise, and chili sauce.

sheesha: a water pipe for smoking tobacco.

shmagh: a man's headcloth, of thicker material than the **ghutra**, and most commonly with a red checkered pattern.

sidr: the nabk tree, growing as high as twelve meters. It has white branches and thorns. It's fruit is edible and camels and goats graze on its leaves. The bark around the roots is used to produce a red dye. It has been said that the **sidr** menstruates like a woman as a result of a red substance that is emitted from the hollows on its surface.

tagiya: a skullcap worn under the **shmagh** or **ghutra**.

thobe: a man's garment, normally white in color and resembling a long shirt that in most cases reaches down to the heel. Some men wear them shorter, above the ankle, and this is seen as a sign of piety.

ulama: religious scholars. In some Muslim countries the **ulama** articulate the official opinion of the religious establishment.

umra: the lesser pilgrimage, which, unlike the Hajj, can take place at any time of year, and can be done in shorter time.

ya: vocative particle, often used in Arabic before someone's name when addressing them.

zakat: the compulsory tax on a Muslim's income that they must pay to the common purse.

zimam: a woman's nose ornament.

Modern Arabic Literature
from the American University in Cairo Press

Bahaa Abdelmegid *Saint Theresa* and *Sleeping with Strangers*
Ibrahim Abdel Meguid *Birds of Amber* • *Distant Train*
No One Sleeps in Alexandria • *The Other Place*
Yahya Taher Abdullah *The Collar and the Bracelet* •
The Mountain of Green Tea
Leila Abouzeid *The Last Chapter*
Hamdi Abu Golayyel *A Dog with No Tail* • *Thieves in Retirement*
Yusuf Abu Rayya *Wedding Night*
Ahmed Alaidy *Being Abbas el Abd*
Idris Ali *Dongola* • *Poor*
Radwa Ashour *Granada*
Ibrahim Aslan *The Heron* • *Nile Sparrows*
Alaa Al Aswany *Chicago* • *Friendly Fire* • *The Yacoubian Building*
Fadhil al-Azzawi *Cell Block Five* • *The Last of the Angels*
Ali Bader *Papa Sartre*
Liana Badr *The Eye of the Mirror*
Hala El Badry *A Certain Woman* • *Muntaha*
Salwa Bakr *The Golden Chariot* • *The Man from Bashmour*
The Wiles of Men
Halim Barakat *The Crane*
Hoda Barakat *Disciples of Passion* • *The Tiller of Waters*
Mourid Barghouti *I Saw Ramallah*
Mohamed Berrada *Like a Summer Never to Be Repeated*
Mohamed El-Bisatie *Clamor of the Lake* • *Drumbeat*
Houses Behind the Trees • *Hunger*
A Last Glass of Tea • *Over the Bridge*
Mahmoud Darwish *The Butterfly's Burden*
Tarek Eltayeb *Cities without Palms*
Mansoura Ez Eldin *Maryam's Maze*
Ibrahim Farghali *The Smiles of the Saints*
Hamdy el-Gazzar *Black Magic*
Fathy Ghanem *The Man Who Lost His Shadow*
Randa Ghazy *Dreaming of Palestine*
Gamal al-Ghitani *Pyramid Texts* • *The Zafarani Files* • *Zayni Barakat*
Tawfiq al-Hakim *The Essential Tawfiq al-Hakim*
Yahya Hakki *The Lamp of Umm Hashim*
Abdelilah Hamdouchi *The Final Bet*
Bensalem Himmich *The Polymath* • *The Theocrat*
Taha Hussein *The Days* • *A Man of Letters* • *The Sufferers*
Sonallah Ibrahim *Cairo: From Edge to Edge* • *The Committee* • *Zaat*
Yusuf Idris *City of Love and Ashes* • *The Essential Yusuf Idris*
Denys Johnson-Davies *The AUC Press Book of Modern Arabic Literature*
In a Fertile Desert: Modern Writing from the United Arab Emirates
Under the Naked Sky: Short Stories from the Arab World
Said al-Kafrawi *The Hill of Gypsies*

Shmmagh